Love Hurts

j.j. Keller

LYRICAL PRESS
Kensington Publishing Corp.
www.kensingtonbooks.com

Lyrical Press books are published by
Kensington Publishing Corp. 119 West 40th Street New York, NY 10018

First Electronic Edition: September 2010
eISBN-13: 978-1-61650-189-1
eISBN-10: 1-61650-189-8

First Print Edition: September 2010
ISBN-13: 978-1-61650-881-4
ISBN-10: 1-61650-881-7

Printed in the United States of America

Can you ever really trust in love?

Falling in love with her fiancé's best friend is wrong--right? Not in Shania Miller's case it isn't. The man she vowed to marry has a second fiancée and failed to remember her after returning from Iraq. Now, unable to trust in love, she answers lonely hearts calls, saving up enough money to attend a university three hours away from the only home she's known.

Broken hearted, Shania and her son move to Briarwood, Indiana. Struggling financially, she wonders if she'll ever have a complete family--one with a mommy and a daddy for her son--will become a reality?

Mark Hardwick stood silently by as his friend broke Shania Miller's heart. His faith allows him to help Shania, especially after she's abandoned by her fiancé and family. Why then, did he hesitate when she announced her broken engagement and love for him on his wedding day?

Books by j.j. Keller

Jewel Heist
Love Hurts

Published by Kensington Publishing Corporation

This book is dedicated to my mother-in-law, Kathyrn Hahn. Family was everything to her.

Acknowledgements

Special thanks to Ericka Scott, Erin Kellison, and Tes Hilaire for helping me whip the manuscript into shape.

Chapter 1

He fidgeted with the blue tie while glancing out the church's chancery window. Her rusty four-door jerked to a stop in a yellow zone of the parking lot. Shania jumped out of the SUV. Morgan's heart pounded against his rib cage. Strands of brown hair caught in the wind fell from the knot at the nape of her slender neck, as she ran to the other side. The baby "everything" bag flopped against her side as she lifted Justin out of the car seat in the rear. Using tight fists, Justin rubbed his eyes, and then wiped his nose on her shoulder. While massaging his back, she kissed his plump baby cheek. There was no denying Shania Miller was an excellent mother.

A teenage girl wearing pigtails, jeans and a white t-shirt met Shania on the sidewalk near the bell tower. A quick transfer and Justin's mouth opened wide as he struggled to grab his mother, kicking his feet in rebellion. Shania handed the bag to the tiny bit of female, and then kissed Justin's forehead. Smoothing his hair, Shania said something to the youngster. A quick bob of her head toward the chancery window, then the overburdened teen pivoted to walk along the cement path. Shania glanced up and smiled. Love for her exploded inside him.

What had she wanted to say last night at the rehearsal? Her perfect lips drew his attention, making him miss most of her words. Unable to resist, his fingers had caressed her bare shoulder as he released her. He chastised himself for giving in and making the contact. Sometimes doing what was morally correct hurt.

"What are you staring at?" Tom asked from behind him.

Hesitant to look away from the scene below, Morgan glanced at his best man, who was tugging his shirt at the neck. "Shania just arrived."

Tom stared at him, reading him as he always did, and nodded. Morgan could never keep his thoughts hidden from him. "Are you sure you want to go through with this wedding? It's not too late to call it off."

Morgan grimaced. Was he that obvious? A few seconds later Shania rushed through the door and stood stock still, gathering her breath. His plebeian attendants hovered, mouths open, gawking at her. Granted, her sexy body was sheathed in a thin form-fitting dress.

"Leave us alone," he ordered. The guys stopped their incessant ribbing for the first time in two days and dragged their feet toward the door.

Shania took his full attention. Though beautiful before, after giving birth to Justin she'd matured into a sexy voluptuous woman. Unlike her normal jeans and sweatshirt, she'd dressed in a revealing outfit and looked stunning.

Should he call off the wedding as Tom had suggested? No, he and Shania could never be together, too many missed opportunities to become lovers. They would be buddies for life and remain simply friends. He tried to think mundane thoughts and proceeded to recite the Ten Commandments, waiting for her to speak her mind.

She dashed forward and halted within an inch of him. The scent of mint surrounded him, rushing out of her mouth, as she licked her perfect pink lips.

"Don't marry her," she demanded.

"What?" Commandments forgotten, he shook his head in disbelief and wonder.

"Don't marry Patty. Please." She held her left hand to her chest as if to push back the heaves. Her engagement ring was gone. Last month, he'd heard rumors of her returning the diamond to Beck. She should have flung the dull jewel into his face the moment she got it years ago.

Morgan glanced at his three friends holding the door open and obviously listening. He waved his hand, urging them to close the door. "Out!"

The trio, fashionably dressed in black tuxes, eased the entrance closed. Shania twisted a lock of hair which had escaped and tucked it into the sloppy knot.

In the back of his mind, he hoped she'd tell him what he'd longed to hear for the past four years. If she didn't, he needed one last caress, and at his touch, vanilla scent from her soft skin filtered into the air, magnifying his stifled yearning. "Why shouldn't I marry Patty?"

She bit her lip and stared at him. Her tiger eyes, filled with insecurity, grew more golden than usual. "Because…"

"Because?" His heart beat as fast as the second hand of the lopsided grandfather clock in the corner, quick and loud. Another strand of hair had escaped. Wanting to touch the soft lock, he tucked it behind her ear.

She stared into his eyes. "Because I love you, and I think you love me."

"You bitch! I knew I couldn't trust you," Patty's screech came from behind them.

Morgan's focus had been on Shania and her declaration. With great reluctance, he pulled his glance away from Shania. Patty, his bride-to-be, was striding forward like an enraged shrew bent on vengeance.

"Patty, we're in a church. My church." He released Shania's arm and held his hand out to take Patty's.

She shook him off and shoved Shania. "You are nothing but a whore. I'm going to tell everyone about--"

"Stop!" Rage like he'd never experienced raked his body, shaking him to his core. He wanted to box the ears of the woman he'd agreed to marry.

"You're out of the wedding," Patty shouted, pointing at Shania.

"Fine." Shania ran to the door and glanced back. Her doe eyes and trembling lips were highlighted by the stained-glass cross cut in the opening.

Morgan couldn't let her leave. "Wait!"

Her feet grounded, and she lowered her head. His throat tightened. She turned and wrapped shaking hands around the handle. He swallowed and took a step.

"Leave the dress," Patty screamed and blocked Morgan's path.

Shania pivoted and glared. "I wore it to the church. I'll have it dry cleaned and returned."

"No, I need the dress now. My cousin is extra-large. She can fill in for you." Patty lifted her lips, resembling the Joker in a Batman movie.

Shania's body stiffened. Her fists tightened beside her hips. She'd been bold enough to live alone, single, pregnant and self-supportive. Could she defy societal norms and walk out of the church without clothing? He wouldn't allow it and tugged an arm of his jacket.

She reached behind and unzipped the pink and turquoise sequined dress. A few shakes of her hips and the slick material fell to the floor.

Morgan removed his coat and missed her as she slid through the door. Catcalls and whistles streamed down the hallway. He rushed through the massive oak door and glowered at his friends. Shania's white rear flashed around the corner, while a hanger swung on the rack where choir robes were stored.

"She's hot," his best man said. "I want some of that."

"Shut up, Tom," Morgan shot back, then swallowed. He took a deep breath and jerked his jacket over his arm. Slowly, he walked into the room, shut the door and leaned against the wood.

Patty hovered in front of the mirror, messing with her hair. "Has she gone? Do you know she called his morning and claimed her brat had the sniffles and tried to cancel?"

"Yes, she left. Justin's not a brat, and I never want to hear you call my son that again." Morgan ground his teeth, even as he tried to gain control of his emotions. He threw his jacket over the back of a chair and crossed his arms. Justin was his son, and he'd love and protect him with his dying breath.

"You need to get ready, honey. I'll have Becky dress, and we'll start in a few minutes." She stepped to him and kissed his tight lips.

"No!" Despite the inside of his mouth bleeding from biting the skin, he was a forgiving man. He would try to see her point of view and end the farce of a relationship. "Look--"

She smiled. Malice, clear and demonic, glittered from her small eyes. "I meant to tell you, a close friend found out Shania works--"

He knew where she worked and he resented Patty's snobbishness and attack. "The wedding's off." He paused as her mouth dropped open. "Do you want me to tell them?"

"What? Why?" Her face scrunched into her famous tear-releasing mode.

"I can't be married to someone who'd treat another person that harshly. Your behavior was immature and cruel. Although I'll always have a... fondness for you, I can't spend the rest of my life with a woman who can hurt others so easily." Why did he say yes to her proposal in the first place? Because he was lonely and finally realized he couldn't have the woman of his dreams—Shania. He'd almost made the biggest mistake of his life. Glancing through the pane, he observed Shania putting Justin in the car seat. Justin was crying and tossing his feet into the air. A black chorus gown belled out as she ran around the sturdy vehicle and slid onto the driver's seat. She leaned her head against the steering wheel. After a few minutes, she visibly straightened her shoulders.

"You bastard. You're doing her, aren't you?" Patty slapped him. Before she bent to pick up the dress, a snarl crossed her face, wicked enough to send Beelzebub back to his black fire. She ran to the door and turned. Eyes glazed over with unshed tears, she demanded, "If you don't marry me, you're paying for the wedding."

Morgan sat down on a bench by the window, rubbing the sting from Patty's hand imprint on his cheek. He flexed his jaw. Joy at Shania's pronouncement took some of the pain away. Shania loved him. He rubbed his chest, the pounding equal to the rhythm of the organ music filling the chapel.

Find Shania, echoed in his mind. She had to wait for him. He ran out of the chapel, shoved flowers flapping in the wind on the outside staircase banister and down the sidewalk. He glanced both ways. Which way had she gone? Morgan started toward his car. It was decorated with white writing on the windows and cans trailing behind.

"Morgan, where are you going?" Mike asked.

Morgan pivoted to see a line of black-suited friends watching him with confused expressions, except Tom. He had a knowing smile on his square face.

Morgan would go after Shania once he told his family and friends the wedding was canceled.

* * * *

Shania spoke in soothing tones to her son. Face red, hair wet from sweat, he grew tired. His feet stopped striking the car seat and rested. Leaning her head against the window, she took a deep breath. She'd taken a risk and lost. Morgan must not love her the same way she loved him. How could she have read each one of the clues wrong?

She'd met Morgan over four years ago. As a high school senior she'd visited several colleges, but focused on Briarwood University because of its reputation. The school possessed a renowned and outstanding art department. Morgan's roommate, Beck Longview, was the upperclassman assigned to show her honors group around the campus. Beck's talent existed in charcoals and hers in pastel painting. Hmm, so like their individual personalities, Beck's work was sketchy and full of dark inconsistencies while her art covered the canvas completely with beautiful vibrant colors--all or nothing for Shania.

"Together, we'd make a whole artistic genius," Beck whispered in her ear the last day of the orientation. He kissed her, a sweet gentle smooch. She gave him her phone number and climbed in her Jeep to return to Cyan, Indiana. He visited Cyan the next weekend. A pattern formed-- she'd attend Summer Workshops at the university or Beck traveled to Cyan.

Morgan Hardwick was Beck's best friend. When Beck would take Shania to his house in Briarwood, Morgan was always around, either in the kitchen getting a snack or watching TV, or typing a business paper. His presence didn't bother her as much as the way he watched her. His soft green eyes, at times, sparked with humor or a flash of heat would appear before he'd lower his glance. More often than not, Morgan would shift his gaze from Beck to her and a frown would appear. He'd tighten his lips and leave the house or shut himself into his bedroom. At the time, Shania considered Morgan's behavior odd and rude.

One August evening, Beck and Shania walked hand in hand down Market Street. Shania glanced toward a couple coming from the opposite direction. Morgan escorted a beautiful blond-haired woman wearing a sheer, knee-length ruby dress. Never having seen him with a date before, Shania's curiosity skyrocketed and she rushed toward them. Morgan's gaze met hers as Beck tugged her arm, causing her to stumble over her feet as he jerked her through the open door of an antique store.

Why hadn't Beck wanted her to meet the lady in red? More importantly, why had she felt compelled to talk with her? Shania's interest in Morgan existed back then--if only she had recognized the attraction. If time could be reversed, she'd have taken a different path. Perhaps she and Morgan could have developed an intimate-love-relationship.

She'd never seen Morgan with the same woman again, and Beck refused to answer Shania's numerous questions about who she was. Recently, the Briarwood newspaper had a wedding announcement--the same woman Morgan had escorted down the sidewalk was getting married to Beck Longview.

Shania huffed. Had Beck been betrothed to the other woman back then? Shania glanced in the rear view mirror to see Justin had settled down. She accelerated to pull out of the church parking lot and braked.

Her affection for Morgan hadn't struck like a white lightning as it had with Beck--no, her love for Morgan had grown over the years. She'd always care for Beck, but this bond with Morgan was solid and everlasting. If she did indeed have an attachment to him. Goodness. Could she have confused a friendship for adoration?

Regardless, neither man was in her life. Her chest tightened and her breath shortened. Her second chance at love failed. Maybe she didn't deserve a happily-ever-after.

Chapter 2

A few blocks later, Shania pulled into the free clinic parking lot. She jumped from the car and opened the rear door. Justin's hair had matted to his head. His cries had converted into mumbling. Could his misery be a result of the upheaval in their lives? Morgan hadn't been around as much, and Justin was accustomed to seeing him several times a week. Their belongings were packed, ready to move, which could be making him insecure.

"Mommy's going to get help for you, baby doll." She unsnapped his seatbelt, wiped the tears drying on his chubby cheeks, placed the carry-all on her shoulder and tugged him out of the car seat. The choir robe's sleeves billowed out, and his arm got caught inside.

She'd grabbed the garment off of a clothes rack in the church seconds after she'd dropped her bridesmaid's dress. Patty's true personality had come to center stage. How long would their marriage last? Probably forever. Morgan was that kind of guy. A sincere, loyal, honest, loving man and she'd let him slip away. Inaction, procrastination and unwarranted loyalty to Beck added up to her losing a good man and, after today, possibly her best friend.

She bit her lip to keep the pain from escaping. Tears welled in her eyes, ready to burst at the first moment of solitude.

Shania rolled the robe's material from Justin's arm. She carried him into the clinic and stopped in front of the desk. "Hi, I'm Shania Miller and this is my son, Justin. I need to have a doctor look at him, please. He's got a temperature and a rash."

The receptionist's brown-eyed gaze rolled over Shania's black gown to her bright turquoise high heels. She glanced at Justin who'd smashed his face into Shania's shoulder. "Have you been here before?"

"Yes, for the past three years."

The woman slipped papers onto a clipboard and handed it through the cutout in the clear plastic shield to Shania. Justin's nose leaked. Shania held the silver clamp and tucked the board under her arm. Juggling Justin and the bag, she took a seat on one of the blue metal chairs in the waiting room. She grabbed a tissue hanging from the outside pocket of the carry-all, then swiped the soft paper under his nostrils. The forms slid off the satin of the robe and onto the floor with a clatter.

She picked it up, drawing in the antiseptic scent of the room. "Justin, I'm going to place your foot on this paper. Okay?"

He nodded. His tiny red nose and sad blotchy face pulled at her heartstrings.

She placed his sneaker on the clipboard and proceeded to fill in the squares. Finished, she moved his foot from the holder and set the completed forms on the next seat. His shoe came loose and fell to the chair. She removed the other one and stuffed both in the bag. She kissed the top of his head, inhaling the baby shampoo mixed with sweat, and snuggled him closer to her. His head rested on her shoulder, the rounded collar of the gown clutched in his fist.

"Scott," the receptionist shouted.

The only other person in the room--Ms. Scott, she assumed--was a short thin woman with gray hair. Worry lines, which were quickly becoming deeply embedded wrinkles, made up the map of a difficult life. Skirt hitting her ankles, she meandered toward the hallway in scuffed penny loafer shoes. She stopped in front of Shania and Justin and smiled, a sad 'I'm sorry you're here' smile. "I'll take your forms to Nurse Ratchet if you wish."

Shania glanced at the glowering nurse standing in the doorway and handed the clipboard to Ms. Scott. "Thank you."

Justin released the robe and rubbed his eyes. He plopped his head onto her shoulder and clasped the material again as if to never let go.

Shania stroked his tiny back and finger-combed his bright blond hair, the exact shade of Beck's. Justin pouted, exhibiting Beck's perfectly shaped lips and stubborn jaw line. Justin's eyes were a green with a starburst of blue shooting from the center, granted to him from her side of the family. A replica of her smaller nose and high cheekbones finished off his precious face.

Having sex with Beck was a violent and painful life changing event, but she'd never regretted conceiving Justin. Her baby was the center of her universe. She'd never let him down like her family had her.

"Dr. Raimo will see you now, Miss Miller," Nurse Ratchet announced in her haughty tone.

Shania placed her chin on top of Justin's head to keep him from bouncing forward and stood. She snagged the handle of the bag and walked down the hallway. The nurse stood in front of an open door. Shania slipped through, placed her sack beside the navy metal visitor's chair, and sat down. The medicinal scent from the sterilized metal equipment made her want to sneeze. She turned her head and sneezed into the loose material of the gown.

Dr. Adam Raimo stood in the doorway a few minutes later, flipping through Justin's chart. He snapped the pages down and a smile appeared on his round face. His teeth were bright, perfectly straight. Dark brown hair curled slightly around his ears. He'd been their doctor since her first pregnancy visit. An obstetrician delivered Justin, but Dr. Raimo examined her baby. They had been partners in Justin's health ever since. "Hi, Dr. Raimo." She shifted Justin around, placing him face out.

"Hi, Miss Miller." His long fingers touched the side of Justin's face, then his forehead. "Buddy, you have a bit of a fever. What else is bothering you?"

"I'm sick," Justin whined and turned his face into her chest again.

"Let's take a look." He patted the cot, paper crinkling as he did.

Shania stood and placed Justin on the white covered examination bed and lifted his shirt. "He has a red rash. I thought it was from the heat, but now there are tiny white dots."

"Sleeping much?" He turned Justin's head side to side.

"No, and he's had a fever for the past two days. This is the third day"

"Does his urine smell?" He continued to search, thumping this and that and looking inside Justin's ears with a rubber funnel.

"Just a little stronger than usual. He's good at drinking water and juice. Liquids generally aren't an issue." She helped Justin to lie on the cot, positioning him for the doctor's examination. "Could it be measles?"

Dr. Raimo lifted an eyebrow. "Has he been around anyone with measles?"

"Yes, a child at the playground had measles a week or so ago." She clenched her fist.

"Unlikely, because his MMR shots are up to date. Justin, we're going to remove your pants and look at your legs, okay?" Dr. Raimo asked.

"No," Justin hooted.

"Don't ask a three-year-old a question and expect yes as the answer, unless it involves toys, play or food." She smiled.

Dr. Raimo grinned and slid the elastic-banded pants off Justin. Justin twisted and turned, trying to avoid contact, but his socks followed. No rash was visible on Justin's legs. The primary points of the red welts were under his arms, neck and back.

When the doctor tickled Justin's feet, they reacted as normal, curling into tight balls. Dr. Raimo replaced the pants and the socks. "Now, Justin, I'm going to sit you up so I can listen to your heart and lungs."

Dr. Raimo caught her glance and nodded. Shania set Justin upright on the padded bench and spoke nonsense words into his ear. Justin closed his eyes, until the stethoscope touched skin, then he jerked backward.

"Sorry, let me warm it." Dr. Raimo blew on the round dial. His breath flowed across the table. Spearmint surrounded them. He unbuttoned his white jacket and rubbed the metal against the linen of his black shirt. The material made his brown eyes darken to a solid walnut color.

He touched the stethoscope to Justin's chest. "Better?"

Justin nodded.

Dr. Raimo moved the device around to Justin's sides, and then to his upper and lower back.

"Well?" she asked, impatient to find out what was wrong with her son.

"You can put his shirt on." He held Justin's tiny hand in his large one. "Good job, Justin."

Dressed, Justin latched onto her, like a chimp holding onto his cage. His heels dug into her sides.

"From the examination, he appears to have roseola, but I want to check for anemia."

Shania dropped onto the visitors' chair, crushed Justin to her chest, feeling his heart beat against hers. Her throat closed off.

"Shoot." Dr. Raimo sat on his wheeled stool and slid it closer to her. "I should have explained what roseola is before I mentioned a blood test."

He placed his hand on Justin's back. "Roseola is similar to measles. The virus lasts two to four days. His temperature can be treated with acetaminophen or cool water and you'll want to take a fever seriously. The symptoms are a pain for the patient and the caretaker."

"So, he'll be all right by tomorrow then?" Her breath hitched.

"As long as he's kept in a comfortable, quiet environment and you watch his fever, he'll be fine. If his temperature keeps rising, you'll need to take him to the ER."

"Quiet?" She closed her eyes and opened them again.

"Yes, will that be a problem?" He dropped his hand, pressed a button on the wall, then picked up the documents.

"No. Yes. It's just we're moving to Briarwood at seven tomorrow morning. I've scheduled movers." She bit her lip. What to do? She couldn't jeopardize Justin's health.

"Do you have anyone to watch him while you get settled?"

"No. No one to help me." She leaned into the hard chair, then situated Justin to cuddle him like a baby. He didn't resist.

"Are you going to the university?"

Her neck twisted as she jerked to look at him. How did he know she was going to college? She quickly replayed conversations they'd had in the past before she drew wrong conclusions. The last time she took Justin for immunizations, she'd told him she'd been taking distance education classes. She smiled. "Yes, I've taken all of the courses online that I can. Now, I get to enter the classroom to practice and learn."

"Congratulations. You'll be finished in four semesters?" He smiled, and then tapped his pen on the counter top.

"Yes. In fifteen months, I'll have a degree."

Nurse Ratchet walked in. Dr. Raimo said something softly to her, then opened the door. "Nurse Treason is new with the clinic. She'll take a sample. Don't worry, she's fantastic with children. In a few minutes, I'll be back to discuss the results with you."

"Thank you." Shania bit into her lip, hard enough to break her hide. For the first time she'd witness a needle pressing into her son's skin, extracting blood. The idea made her wish it was her receiving the puncture.

"Justin, I'm going to put this rubber band thing around your arm so I can get a good vein. Here we go, this is going to sting a little." Nurse Treason's voice was soft and comforting. She seized his arm, wrapped the tourniquet, swiped an alcohol-scented tiny square over a patch of skin and inserted the syringe. Not a jab, but a gentle easing of the tiny pinpoint under his pale flesh. Justin tried to jerk his arm, but she held it steady. The glass tube filled with his blood, and she released the tourniquet and then eased the needle out. A second later a Snoopy Band-Aid covered the pinprick.

"There you go, little guy." She tapped his leg and shuffled through the door. Her bedside manner with children was much better than with adults. She was instantly removed from the Nurse Ratchet category.

Shania glanced at her son. Why hadn't he cried?

He looked at his arm. His lips quivered, shaking until his mouth opened and a scream vibrated from deep in his throat. She shot off the chair, placed Justin's head near her neck and walked back and forth bouncing as she went. The large sleeves of the choir robe flowed out. The smooth satin rubbed against her bare legs. Soon, his wails subsided to sniffles.

"There now, you're such a brave boy. I'm so proud of you." She rubbed small circles on his back. Several minutes later he fell asleep. Tiny hiccups escaped as he breathed.

Shania settled onto the hard chair and snuggled Justin. Bile had risen to her throat. She swallowed, trying to send the vile liquid back to her stomach.

Twenty minutes passed before Dr. Raimo reentered the examination room. She pierced him with a stare, trying to determine if the news was good or bad.

He sat down and wheeled the chair inches from her. Her heart stopped beating. No breath could get past her throat. No, it could not be bad news. Justin was the only constant good thing in her life. Please God, he had to spare her son.

Dr. Raimo touched her hand, which was resting on Justin's back. "All of his blood results came back in good form. Although he's older than the typical patient he hasn't had a lot of exposure to childhood illnesses to boost his immunities. I'm confident that's what it is, considering he was at the playground with another kid who may have had it. I could run a test for roseola antibodies, but I don't think it's necessary."

She released a puff of air. Her heart, having shut off, started pounding again. "Thank you."

"Nurse Treason is getting care instructions for you." He hesitated. "I hope you don't mind my asking a personal question."

He smiled, grooves along the sides of his mouth grew deeper. Odd that he'd asked her first instead of just blurting out the question, as he had when inquiring about Justin's father. She didn't have any medical secrets from him.

She nodded.

"Actually two questions."

"Go ahead," she responded.

"Did Justin's father ever get released from the rebels' camp in Iraq? And why are you wearing a choir robe with glittery high heels?" He nodded to her shoes.

She imagined he expected two totally different answers, but they were related. "I want to answer your questions, but first I need a drink of water."

"Of course. Come with me into the doctor's lounge. We'll talk in private." He grabbed her bag.

Shania stood with an exhausted Justin asleep and drooling on her shoulder.

The door opened and Nurse Treason shuffled in, a frown marring her sharp-featured face.

"We'll be down the hall. Is that her paperwork?" He snatched the pages from her fingers. "Miss Miller's the last patient for the day, right?"

"Yes." She lifted her long nose a pinch and shook her head. Gray curls sprung into action as she did, bouncing back and forth like miniature accordions. "Where are you going?"

Shania glanced at him.

He smiled and one-arm-hugged the nurse. "Don't worry about it, we're not going far."

Out the door and a few steps later, they entered a bright, sun-filled room.

"This is our consultation room slash doctor's room. We want it to be comfortable for our clients." He held out a hand. "Have a seat."

Khaki cloth cushions, three-inches-thick, covered the six foot sofa. It was flanked by two padded metal blue chairs. A small refrigerator had been stashed near the coat rack. She took a seat on a couch. He took a step toward the cold bin and opened the white door.

His large fingers clasped two bottles. Uncapping one on this way back to the area, he situated the water on a small square coaster, on the tile top of the table on her left.

Dr. Raimo sat down in a chair near her, rolled the lid off a bottle and took a deep drink.

"Now, what's going on in Shania's world? Did your fiancé return from war? He was part of M triple A, Mortars, Artillery and Attack Aviation, right?" He crossed his leg and braced a hand on his ankle. He wasn't wearing a wedding band. She hadn't noticed before, but coming from Morgan's ceremony had created awareness. Had Morgan said "I do"?

"Are you married?" she blurted out.

"No, though I'd like to settle down sometime soon. Back to you." He smiled and removed the stethoscope from around his neck. The metal end clanked against the sand-colored tile.

"Yes, Beck, the sperm donor, was rescued and released from active duty. He's under supervised care at this time. He has an adjustment problem called post-traumatic stress disorder."

"Shania, PTSD is an anxiety disorder, not an adjustment problem."

The instant Beck returned from the hospital, his parents told her to break the engagement because he'd never recover. It took her several months to believe them. Now she realized that they'd lied all along. In her mind, during their intimacy she and Beck had become one and she couldn't abandon him in his time of need. Love was fleeting, as she'd discovered, because Morgan was exchanging vows with another.

Justin shifted, resting more comfortably.

"I see." Shania glanced at Dr. Raimo. "Is it normal for him to go to sleep so suddenly? He's had sporadic rest in the last few days."

"Yes, eventually the body shuts down. He's actually at the end of his roseola. The raised dots should start to disappear."

She nodded and finger-combed Justin's hair. It was comforting to talk about her past and for some reason felt compelled to continue. "The trauma of the terrorist interrogation has affected Beck. He's changed."

"There have been a lot of cases of PTSD, military personnel in Iraq, most who learn to manage the illness incurred while on duty." He lowered his leg and leaned forward. The interest in his eyes mixed with his sympathetic tone.

"Yes, the doctors said the same thing. Except it's not just the illness. I don't have the same feelings for Beck. I'm not sure we can even be friends." She witnessed the pity in Dr. Ramio's eyes and lowered her glance to the floor. She didn't want or need sympathy. Her folks choose not to support her. Beck's parents denied Justin as their grandson. Townspeople believed she was a whore. And the man she truly loved was marrying another woman. Commiseration was the last thing she needed.

"A month ago I ended our engagement, which was best for both of us. I'm going to finish school. Justin and I will begin again." She loosened Justin's shirt from under his arm where the fabric had wrinkled during the fidgeting.

"Shania?" Dr. Raimo whispered.

She glanced at him, shocked at his using her given name with an intimate tone. Should she run or stay and hear him out? The nurse remained outside, right?

"You've done nothing wrong. You're an excellent mother to an amazingly bright boy. Accomplishing as much as you have with such limited resources should make people clap in your honor, not shun you." His brown eyes held sincerity and another emotion she couldn't place.

Heat rose to her face. In the past three years, she hadn't heard praise, other than from Morgan. "Thank you."

"Since Justin's no longer my patient, I'll tell you something personal about me."

Her chest restriction lightened because of his compliment. Her cheeks didn't burn as much as they had a moment ago. She shook her head. Had he said Justin wasn't his patient anymore? "Are you dumping us?"

"No. Well, in a way. I'm going to be a professor in the Medical Center at the university. We'll both be on campus. Perhaps we could get together for coffee sometime?" He smiled and pulled a white business card from his lab coat.

She'd had very little sleep the last several days and the drama today made her uncomprehending. "You're moving to Briarwood?"

"Yes, in three weeks. I want to teach and help pave the way for new physicians." He wrote on the blank side of the paper. "Now, tell me about the robe. Why are you wearing a choir gown with glittery shoes?"

"Remember my friend Morgan? He came with me when Justin had check-ups?"

He nodded and tucked the pen into his jacket pocket.

"He's getting married today, and I was to be in the wedding. Because of Justin's illness, I tried to get out of going to the ceremony but Morgan's fiancée can be very intimidating." She tucked a curl behind her ear. Her chest continued to ache.

"Bridezilla?"

She grinned. "At the least." A sigh escaped. "I made the mistake of telling Morgan not to marry her and she overheard."

"Because?" He leaned forward as if curious to hear.

What was wrong with her, revealing everything to a man she barely knew? He was her son's doctor, not her psychiatrist. She smoothed the cloth of her robe and didn't look at his face. She had to hide the grief and love for the man she'd left in the church chapel. "I had my reasons."

Shania readjusted Justin's weight and snuck a peek at Dr. Raimo. His eyes held sadness. Would he think her pathetic, asking another man to not marry his bride minutes before he was to say I do? Probably. It sounded very bad in her head right now.

Dr. Raimo grinned. "The bridal party was wearing choir robes in the wedding?"

She chuckled. "No. The bride insisted I remove the dress so she could get a replacement on the spot. The robe was the first thing I saw to cover myself." Shania crossed her ankles and took a sip of the cool water. "I wanted immediate help for Justin, so I came here directly."

"They exchanged vows anyway?" He lifted an eyebrow.

Why wouldn't they? The town slut tells a groom on his wedding day she loves him. They'd get a good laugh for months from that one. She leaned her cheek on Justin's shoulder and wiped away her own tear.

"I assume. I removed the dress and ran." She set the water bottle down and glanced at the clock on the wall. "Which I need to do again in order to get ready for the move."

She tucked Justin close and unsteadily rose. Grabbing the bag, she took off at a fast trot toward the door.

Dr. Raimo raced her to the entry. His hand pressed the handle down. Between his fingers he held the business card. "Maybe I'll see you on campus. Here's my card, call me if you need medical help or a referral."

Chapter 3

Justin rested comfortably in his crib. Shania couldn't sleep. She glanced at her cellphone--ten o'clock. Not late by any means, but the movers were scheduled at seven in the morning. Once they arrived in Briarwood, she'd have a long day of unpacking what was necessary. However, most important of all was taking care of Justin.

She walked around the boxes, making sure they were sealed. The rustic golden wall paint looked dingy without artwork to enhance the color. Her lips curved in memory of her and Morgan painting the house. He'd hated the "baby poop" color she'd chosen for the living room until she muted the tone with an amber glaze. Then the ambiance became Tuscan as she'd planned.

Morgan. Her breath held for a few seconds and then started. Had he gone ahead and married Patty? Maybe he'd misunderstood her declaration. Perhaps she shouldn't have run. Could she have stood in front of him wearing only a strapless bra, thong and high heels? No, she'd never exposed her body in public and probably wouldn't have removed the dress if it wasn't for the confidence she'd gained from working at Companion Connections. The job built her self-assurance and as a result she could--would--speak her mind.

As if she had a choice in removing the gown. Wanting to escape an awkward situation, she stepped out of her shell. Thank goodness the choir robes were nearby.

Returning the gown was easier than she'd thought it would be. Shania stopped at a store near Morgan's church to get the special drinks the nurse recommended instead of juice for Justin. A dry cleaner was two doors down. She changed into a pair of shorts and shirt stored in the trunk of her car and dropped off the black chorus gown to be cleaned. Fortunately they did business with the minister and promised to add it to their next order. Thankful, she paid and left, noting the cathedral's parking lot was empty. Two hours had passed since she arrived at the doctor's. A vacant lot wasn't a sign that the wedding had been canceled, but her spirit raised anyway.

Shania closed her eyes, keeping the pain at bay. She walked around the packing crates to the front door and stepped outside into the balmy night, leaving the entrance ajar enough to hear her son. She glanced at the gray rectangle mailbox attached to the cream siding and a sliver of excitement ran through her. Her fingernail slid between the lid and box. Would there be a message from Morgan, stating "I was here, where were you?" She glanced inside. No mail. No love note. No future with Morgan. Deep seated misery made her throat hurt. She leaned her forehead against the frame of the doorway and took a deep breath, resisting the urge to cry. She hadn't cried for Beck when she said goodbye, yet now she wanted to open the gates and flood the last of her tissues.

"Shania?"

She sniffed back the dribble, brushed her nose with the back of her hand and swiveled around. Her gut clenched in agonizing fear. Morgan wore his black tux without the tie and corsage. His shirt had been unbuttoned enough to show a t-shirt beneath. He looked like a movie star in his breathtaking beauty. She loved him. Her breath caught in her throat. He didn't smile. "You look like the newest double oh-seven."

"We need to talk," he responded. He stood in the shadows. She couldn't read his expression, but his tone sounded serious.

The time is now, her mind shouted. *Go for it or lose the chance to connect.* She took a step. Morgan moved out of the darkness. Pain and joy sparkled in his eyes. Shania grabbed his lapels and tugged him closer. "I'd rather claim my first kiss."

Morgan exhaled. His whispered curse hovered near her ear and then was carried away on the wind. He held her gaze, searing her, as if digging deep into her soul. She licked her lips, hoping he wouldn't deny her. Her gaze moved to his mouth, waiting and wishing. She held her breath. Would he? Oh, God, let him dare!

He tilted his head and cupped her face. She closed her eyes and moved an inch, no more, no less. Like an addiction, she needed to feel the heat of his hands. Yet, the slightest move and she'd lose the fragile contact she did have with him. His thumbs rubbed her cheeks, soft tiny brushes.

She released the breath caught in her chest, then pulled her lips inward to wet them again. He smelled like spicy cinnamon and male aftershave. Her gut clenched in agony. His closeness was pleasure and pain. Her knees weakened. Morgan quickly moved his hands from her face to her arms, as if to hold her up.

"Ah, Shania." He pressed his cheek against hers, taking a deep breath. "What are you doing to me? I can't resist you."

"Then don't. I want you. Do you want me?" She begged for his lips to touch hers, just one slight taste of him. One time to test the sparks, to see if a fire would ignite as she'd anticipated.

A lock of her hair, fallen from the loose bun, fluttered as he exhaled. Self doubt crept up her spine. She wouldn't ask again. Either he wanted to be with her or not.

He tugged her close. Her thin t-shirt pressed against the starched suit jacket, causing her nipples to harden. She laid her cheek on his lapel, trying to steady her trembling legs while giving him space and time to come to a decision. The scent of the lily corsage remained on the coat, a quick and painfully sharp reminder that he could very well be married. She sucked in a harsh breath, praying it wasn't true.

"Did you mean what you said?" he whispered. His hands embraced her, his palms resting near her waist with fingers touching the curve of her back. Their thighs touched. Liquid pooled low in her abdomen. She wanted to crawl inside him.

"Every word." Hopeful excitement rang through her slow whispered words.

"Do you want to be together?" He rested his chin on top of her head.

"Yes."

"Then I--"

Justin screamed. Torn between needing to hear Morgan's words and going to her son, she stepped out of his arms. Uncertain, she gazed at Morgan. Was he proposing a future?

Morgan kissed the top of her head. "Go to him."

"Will you be here after I get him settled?" She hated the almost desperate, needy tone creeping into her voice. Tears stung her eyes.

With a slight shake of his head, he whispered, "I'm sorry, Shania…"

Unable to stand listening to the rest of his words, Shania turned and rushed into the house. Their love wasn't meant to be. He'd go do what he felt was necessary and she and Justin would leave for Briarwood.

* * * *

Farmland separated by wooded acres surrounded the mid-size sprawling city of Briarwood, Indiana. Briarwood University was a complex mix of ancient chipped-brick buildings, smelling of time, and oddly angled contemporary structures. The campus was fastidiously perfect with layers of flora. Unique groupings of landscaping were intermeshed with stone statues fitting the area--frogs near the ponds, a Native American in the history quad, a couple walking hand in hand near the dormitories. The fragrant outdoor scents took Shania's breath away each time she visited, as the lovely smells had earlier today as she meandered along the pathways.

The areas of the college grounds were identified according to the plant scheme. West Quad consisted of nutty oaks, pecans and fat-branched, big-leaved blackwood trees. Strategically placed benches allowed visitors a view of the beautiful wooded area. North Quad consisted of lush tickle grass, day lilies and elderberry bushes, while South Quad hosted boxwoods shaped into cones, rectangles and circles. Shania and Justin lived in a family housing complex on the East side, in one of the ancient buildings.

The East Quad was Monet colorful. Riverside Avenue hosted a line of brownstone buildings with newer high rise modern-day housing units behind the rustic structure. Worthen Complex had the oldest and least expensive apartments, primarily because of their small size. Despite the pain of carrying a stroller and baggage to the fifth floor, she loved her living space and wouldn't go to the ground level even if a unit opened. They resided on the west end. Each night a fabulous evening sun filtered through the paned windows. The original brick sill outlined the casing, and a set of gargoyles held sentry on the cement ledge outside the structure. One of the mythological creatures shadowed the glass outside their bedroom. His heavy presence was visible through the living room window as well.

Shania glanced through the dark panes, unable to sleep. Her job with Companion Connections had run from eight in the evening to two the next morning. Although she and Justin had been in Briarwood for three months she missed talking to lonely people on the phone late at night. Her internal clock hadn't adjusted to being able to rest at regular intervals. However, she couldn't continue to keep late hours in addition to rising early in the morning to attend class. Somehow she had to find a way to snooze.

"Mommy," Justin screamed.

She rushed to his side. He was tightly bound in his covers and sweat coated his face. "You're wrapped up like the mummy we saw in the museum. Remember how we laughed at his costume?"

"No." His lips quivered.

"I'm here, honey." She cuddled him close and stroked his back. The nightmares continued. At first she had assumed the dreams were a result of uprooting him from the only home he'd known, or sleeping in the new child bed instead of a crib. Instead, the changes in their lifestyles, class, daycare and Justin being separated from her for long periods created anxiety for him.

"The monster's getting me." He nuzzled his face into her nightshirt.

"What monster?" She glanced around the room, trying to figure out what odd shape would create a scary image for him. Maybe he continued to worry over the mummy.

"There." He pointed toward the window.

"The statue?" Gauzy curtains covered the panes allowing sunlight and moon light to filter in, making the room seem larger. Beyond the glass was the concrete gargoyle, holding court over students gathering in the yard below.

He nodded.

"Why, that's Morgan the second, here to watch over us. He's not a monster. He loves us and sits outside on the cement ledge to keep strangers away. We'll call him M-two." Shania rocked Justin, gently humming a song and making up the words as she went along.

The peaked ears and heavy coat mantle of the stone statue were clearly defined and created exaggerated shadows on the wall.

"Okay. I want him."

She rubbed her cheek against his. She missed Morgan too. They'd seen him at least twice a week for the past three years. He'd spend hours playing with Justin and chatting with her. They hadn't seen nor heard from Morgan since his wedding day several weeks ago. His absence was noticeable and heartrending.

"I do too, honey." Her voice came out as low and as sad as she felt.

She moved Justin's new toddler bunk to the other side and her bed near the window. As the bed legs dragged on the hardwood floor, loud shrill squeaks resonated in the bedroom. Shania could only hope the neighbors were deep sleepers. Shania and Justin had painted a colorful country scene on a canvas last Sunday to use as wall art. Justin loved horses, so they were at the forefront of the picture. Shania hung the canvas between the beds giving him a little more privacy.

Justin finally rested. Shania pressed her face against the windowpane and glanced at the gargoyle, nestled in the mossy green bed on the cement ledge. "Please keep better guard over us, M-two."

She pivoted to walk into the compact living room. Open concept or not, the space was miniature compared to the old house she'd rented in Cyan. She did like how the kitchen incorporated a breakfast bar. However, with no space for a dining table, she and Justin had developed the bad habit of eating in front of the television. Someday, post-school, she'd get a job in a museum or work in an art studio, and hopefully earn enough money to get them a house with two bedrooms and a dining room. Right this moment she had to worry about getting by until her next CD payout. She sighed.

The next morning as she finished packing her book bag, she picked up her phone and pressed Morgan's speed dial number. Before the call rang twice, she ended the connection. What would she say to him? "Hey, how do you like married life?" No, asking about his marriage to a woman who made her strip and leave a church in her underwear was a silly reason to call. Shania had to think of something substantial.

A sigh slipped from her as she glanced toward the bedroom. Justin wasn't a morning person, preferring to sleep in and stay up late at night. Each morning he became a grumpy bear. She placed cereal in his favorite Diego and Dora bowl, added milk and replaced the half gallon in the nearly empty refrigerator. Routine activity would provide a sense of order. She needed the comfort of ordinary and separated the pulp from the orange juice. The few dribbles of the liquid went into a matching Diego sippy-cup. Procrastination was one of her weakness, so she arranged the dishes on the placemat and then strutted toward her adorable beast.

They always decided what clothes Justin wanted to wear the night before, and then placed them on the dresser in preparation. She leaned over him and smoothed a long lock to the side of his face. He resembled Beck in appearance and Morgan in attitude, mannerisms and personality. Sometimes Justin could be very stubborn and like his role model, Morgan, grit his teeth while placing his hands on his hips. A sharp ache tore at her chest. So much pain had occurred in the past three years.

"Justin, baby doll, it's time to get up." Her fingers created circles on his arm.

He yawned and snuggled down farther.

"Sister Agnes is waiting." She ruffled his hair.

"No," he responded.

"I need to go to class. Up! I have your favorite cereal," she firmly stated.

His head popped from under the covers. "Crunch?"

Shania nodded.

He threw off the covers and climbed off the bed.

"Need help with the bathroom activities?"

"No. Big boy." He yawned.

"That's right. I don't have a baby doll anymore. I have a big boy."

He nodded and covered a yawn. Then, he shuffled out of the bedroom and into the bath. Sometimes she missed her baby, because he certainly was becoming a big boy.

* * * *

October continued to be warm, to Shania's pleasure. Patterns formed-- Class, daycare, study. Sometimes her personal preferences didn't fit well into the professor's schedule. Today was one of those days. The lecture ran over by fifteen minutes. Frantic, she hoisted her portfolio onto her shoulder and rushed to pick up Justin. The pain in her chest seemed more intense today, causing her breath to catch, and not because of running from the classroom. No, the ache had been present from the time she'd left Morgan at the church.

Would she ever be able to breathe normally again?

"Shania. Shania Miller." A man's deep voice rushed the words. A bit of anxiousness filtered through his tone.

She didn't want to stop. Justin's keen sense of timing made her run a little faster. Justin would worry.

"Wait up, Shania," he shouted.

She sighed and pivoted a half-turn. "Dr. Raimo."

Dressed in a dark blue polo and khakis, he approached her with a broad smile. She held out her hand, causing the portfolio to bang against her side. He was handsome, smart and kind, but her heart belonged to Morgan. Dr. Raimo wanted a friendship, but if he had more than that in mind, she'd have to refuse an invitation. There wasn't room for their lives for a prospective lover or father figure. However, he was a sweet man, so out of respect she'd be nice and listen.

His dark brown irises lit with a fire as she looked into his eyes. Crap, the guy was into her.

He clasped her hand. Peppermint-scented breath rushed out in short puffs. "Shania, how are you doing? Classes going well?"

"Yes. I'm sorry, I need to go. I have to get Justin from daycare." Her hand slipped from his grip. His eyes opened wide, no doubt because of her impolite behavior. She turned, her sneakers squeaking on the linoleum, hurried out the door and trotted down the sidewalk. She'd have to add rudeness to her growing list of unattractive qualities.

Two blocks later, she walked through the open oval oak door into the vestibule of the church. The scent of sage and frankincense assaulted her nostrils as it had each time she'd entered. One antique walnut staircase and three turns down a hallway later, she came to the lower level nursery.

She peeked through the clear round pane. Her son sat at a child sized table drawing with crayons.

A rectangular face surrounded by white and black cloth obscured the window. Thick lenses enlarged dark irises in the deep set eyes. Shania jumped, her hand flying to her chest. The door opened. Sister Agnes's large caped figure filled the space. Her beaded rosary swung out as she moved her generous hips. She was a force, and currently she blocked the entry.

"Miss Miller, you've come to collect your son?" Her whispered voice carried to Justin.

His face lit, and he scrambled from the table. Shania's heart filled with happiness.

"Yes, I'm sorry I'm late. The class ran over." Shania's voice rang through the room.

"Some children are napping. Please keep your voice lowered." Sister Agnes's jowls jiggled like a bulldog's.

"Sorry, Sister," Shania softly responded as she stepped across the threshold.

Justin stowed his crayons and stuffed his miniature artist pad in his backpack. He rushed to her side.

"Miss Miller, I find it necessary to mention that Justin's shoes don't fit his feet properly. The mission store is open if you'd like to take a look." Her nose turned down, allowing her to peer over her tiny square spectacles.

"Thank you, Sister, I'll do that." Shania grabbed Justin's wrist. They made their way to the door. A roar filled her ears as her breath caught. The tears would have to wait. She refused to show weakness in public.

She held tight to Justin's hand, exited the room and turned the corner. Up a small set of stairs she entered the *Gently Used* store. The scent of starch and buffed old leather assaulted her nostrils.

"Hi, Sister Magdalene. I'm searching for a pair of shoes for Justin. Has anything come in about his size?" Shania asked, while glancing at the clothing. Soon she'd have to buy him a new winter coat. The truth was she couldn't purchase anything until her Certificate of Deposit matured in two weeks. In a moment of brilliance, she'd placed money in a number of CDs. Her research proved the deposits were a safe and efficient way of saving money. She made sure they matured at various times. She laughed. It wasn't a well-made plan. Her books ended up costing twice what she'd allowed and between that and various other supplies, now she was strapped for cash.

"I'm sorry, Shania. Shoes go fast, out of the box, onto the shelves and into hands of the needy." She shook her head, making her habit shake. "I do have a fine pair of cowboy boots which might fit Master Justin."

She scurried to a wooden unit supported by bookshelves. Her nimble pale fingers tugged a lonesome pair of child's red leather boots off the last rack. A bronco rider, with a lasso spinning above his head, had been stitched on the front of each shoe.

"Oh," Justin said. His face lightened with joy. He loved horses and there they were, ready to be worn and admired every day.

"Want to try them on, Justin?" Sister Magdalene's moon-shaped face brightened the room.

He nodded, his blond locks falling into his eyes.

Sister Magdalene sat on the floor and waved him over. He immediately ran, pivoted and sat on her lap. She pulled off the too-tight footwear and slipped on the boot. The left shoe hit the floor with a thud and the second cowboy rider was secured in place.

"Now then, give them a try."

Justin stood and clomped around a small section of flooring. They were too big.

"Mommy?" His anxious, sweet face begged her to take them.

"The way he's been growing, Shania, they'll fit in a few weeks. They're gently used." Sister Magdalene rose, grabbed a red bandana, and wrapped it around Justin's neck. She directed him to stand in front of the mirror.

He was adorable. Too bad Halloween had passed. "How much are they?"

"Five dollars." The sister smoothed Justin's hair. "The bandana is a gift."

Shania could eat peanut butter sandwiches for a few nights and Justin loved cereal. Thirteen more days and she'd have cash once again.

"We'll take them." She smiled at Justin who proceeded to whoop and clack around the space, swaggering like a cowboy. "Thank you, Sister."

Her fingers dug through her backpack, searching the four pockets and coming up empty. Finally, in the center, tucked in a small space, was the five dollar bill. She laid it on the counter. The ting of the antique cash register sounded as the drawer popped out. Shania picked up his tennis shoes. He'd want to wear the boots home today.

The time it took to get back to their apartment doubled as he slipped and slid on the oversized footwear. She couldn't deny him the pleasure of owning the waders, and his small toes deserved a break.

* * * *

The next day Sister Agnes opened the door to the nursery with a frown on her wrinkled face. Crap, she didn't look happy. The news would not be good.

"Miss Miller, Justin has been complaining of his feet hurting." Large knuckled fingers shoved glasses higher on her age-spotted nose.

"I'm sorry, Sister. Not to make excuses, but the mission store didn't have something his size. We did find a pair of boots, but they're too large. I'll buy him a pair of shoes in a few days. Until then, can he wear slippers to school?" Heat rushed to her face. She tried to tell herself she was a good mother, a good provider. Her shoulders slumped forward. She hadn't planned very well.

"If cash is a problem we have a fund for indigents. We'll ask Father Michael to give you some money to buy him shoes." Sister Agnes's foul breath flowed over Shania's face.

"No," Shania barked.

The nun took a step back. Her pale trembling fingers grabbed the cross on her rosary.

Justin ran forward, a frown on his face. Hands on his hips he faced Sister Agnes.

"I'm sorry, Sister. I can take care of my son. It's simply a matter of timing." She shrugged. "His feet grew too fast and my money is tied up in a CD. In twelve days the first thing I'll buy will be shoes."

Shania held her arm across her stomach. Self-doubt sent a horrible ripping cramp through her, chilling her. She could provide for her son and she would.

"Shania." Her voice was firm and low.

Shania lifted her glance to meet Sister Agnes's dark gaze.

"Normally we don't reduce fees, although I think we can in this one case. You only bring Justin for one hour and thirty minutes on Friday. Why don't you talk to your friends, see if they can watch him during that class time? You'll be paying twenty dollars less a week." She dropped the cross then touched the side of Shania's face. "You're a good mother. You provide excellent care for your son."

"Thank you, Sister." She grabbed Justin's hand. "I'll see what I can do."

Outside the church she lifted Justin. Guilt-ridden, she carried him home. "Please, God, will this struggle ever end?"

Chapter 4

Thursday was the longest day of the week for Shania. She rushed from class to class until three, then she scampered to daycare to collect Justin. At five-thirty a teen from down the hall came to watch him until ten, when Shania arrived home from night class. Friday became her day of freedom. She only had one session, drawing with Monsieur Barrett. The last day of the week would be the one she could keep Justin out of daycare.

Between her Thursday class sessions, she hurried to the Fine Arts building and tapped on Monsieur Barrett's office door.

"Come in," he bellowed. That deep baritone voice coming from such a small man always set her on edge.

Shania cracked the door open. "May I have a moment, sir?"

"Yes, of course, Shania. Come in." He smiled and pointed to the seat opposite his massive walnut desk. She opened the door wider and shuffled to the hard wooden chair.

"Sir, I'm seeking your help. Do you remember a student from four years ago, Beck Longview?" She smoothed down her slacks, wiping the sweat from her palms. Reluctant to seek help, she forced herself to ask for this small grant from her professor, lessening her pride a little. One of her positive traits was persistence. She wouldn't give up until the professor granted her wish. However, the process wasn't easy. Her glands went into overdrive. Sweat trickled down her back and she needed to pee.

He tugged on his white goatee and pursed his lips. "Yes, I do, excellent with charcoals. One of my best students. His parents are funding the new art museum on Bell Street. In his honor, I believe."

"Yes, the very ones." Resentment rippled through her. The Longviews' rejection of Justin continued to hurt her. The art museum was three stories of decadent pretentiousness. Was the new construction a way of eulogizing Beck?

"Where is Beck now, I wonder?" Monsieur scrapped his whiskers with two fingers, the sound snapping through the silent office.

"He went to Iraq, has PTSD and is now being cared for by his parents." She bit her lip, hating that it was so simple to categorize Beck's life into one negative sentence.

"I'm sorry to hear that. He was brilliant." Hair crept over his big earlobes as he shook his head.

"Yes, he is gifted with drawing." She scooted forward on the chair. "The reason I'm here is to ask if I might bring my--our--three-year-old son to class with me on Fridays." She needed to connect the school's greatest financial contributors, the Longviews, to her son in order to get some leniency. Not something she was proud of, but Justin came first.

Lips tightened and a cloud cast his eyes.

"Before you say no. He's a very well-behaved child. We have three weeks left in the semester. I promise, he won't be an intrusion. He'll only be here for ninety minutes each time."

"No children in the classroom." His jaw firmed. He reached up to pull on an ear lobe.

She'd beg if necessary. "It's difficult being a single mother."

Each day she discovered how her choices influenced her son. Had she made the right decisions? A large tear plopped over her eyelid, hovered on her cheek. She resisted the urge to wipe the moisture away and draw attention to her weakness. "I loved him, and we intended to marry."

"Why didn't you? PTSD isn't crippling, is it?" He waved his hand in a dismissal mode.

Shania glanced to her right as his graduate assistant slowly shut the door. "He was taken hostage and brutally ill-treated. His squad finally helped him to break free from his captors after a year. He's not capable of holding a job or maintaining a regular existence. He doesn't remember me."

Monsieur's eyes clouded with sympathy. She didn't want pity. She needed time. He simply must allow her son to come with her for a few hours during class. This was the only solution. Determined, she'd do what she had to in order to provide a comfortable life for Justin.

"One hour will help me. Psychologically, Justin is still adjusting to being away from me. He's quiet." She twisted her hands together.

"So he's not like his father." The smile wasn't cynical, but touched on humor.

"Just in appearance." She glanced at her watch.

"Okay. We'll try tomorrow. He'll stay in my office. You do not tell the other students he is your son because everyone will want their child, grandchild, niece, et cetera, to join the class. If necessary, I'll tell people he's family. If it doesn't work out--too much noise, or any disturbance-- he'll not be allowed to return." He stood, ending her session.

"Thank you, Professor." She stood and gathered her bags.

"I'll see you later tonight for lecture," he said and opened the door leading into the classroom.

She walked through and glanced around. The only entrances into the room were from his office and the hallway. She could place her easel between the two doors. Justin would be in her line of sight.

Shania ran to her next class, plotting in her mind. The total of sixty dollar daycare savings would provide winter clothes for Justin. He'd grown at such a fast rate none of his cold weather garb fit him. Late November, snow would fall. His lightweight jacket would not suffice.

Class ended without her truly listening to the lecture. In robot mode, she exited the classroom and building. Despite the distractions, she sensed someone following her to the church. A quick glance showed students hustling to classes, home, or wherever. She halted to stare at a pair of lovers entwined on a bench, kissing. A pang of envy ran through her.

They stopped the lip lock and glanced at her. She smiled and hurried toward her destination, heat rushing through her. Several hurried steps later, she ran fingers through her hair, calmed her fast breathing and entered the church.

The portal to daycare creaked open before she could knock. "Miss Miller."

"Sister Agnes, how are you?"

"Quite well, thank you. Justin has been impatiently waiting for you today." Her lips tightened as she folded her hands in front of her portly belly. The cross, secured by rosary beads attached to a belt clasped between the folds of her waist, swung back and forth.

"I've made arrangements for Justin on Fridays, so he won't be here the next three," Shania blurted.

"Very well. I assume you're going to purchase him shoes. A child's feet should not be bound in tight apparel." Her eyes narrowed. The woman had a one track mind.

"No, Sister, they should not. Yes, I certainly will purchase footwear for him as soon as possible." Shania smiled to lessen the sharpness of her tone.

j.j. Keller

Justin rushed to her side holding his backpack and coat in his hands. "Hi, Mommy."

Shania crouched and hugged him close. "Hi, baby doll."

He frowned and cocked an eyebrow. She'd already forgotten not to call him baby.

"Er, I mean, honey. Let me help you." She dropped to her haunches. Her portfolio clanked against the tiled floor.

Justin dropped his bag and slid an arm in his coat. She helped him maneuver his other limb in the sleeve and zipped the jacket. One strap of his backpack was placed on his shoulder and then the other. He was set to go. Shania lifted her portfolio and repositioned her messenger sack.

"Thank you, Sister. We'll see you next Monday." Shania glimpsed a slight shift of the Sister's lips.

"Did you have a nice day?" Shania glanced at Justin as they walked out the front of the church.

"Yes, Jeremy barfed. It was gross." Justin made gagging noises.

Great. She hoped Jeremy didn't have the flu. "How about peanut butter and jelly sandwiches for dinner?"

"Umm, okay." He ran to the three-tier fountain in the square and leaned over. The angel at the top poured the water from an urn, which spiraled over a ball, and dripped onto a half-moon. From there the fluid drained to a round bowl which splashed out into a larger basin.

"Penny?" Justin glanced into the water.

Coins shimmered under the clear water. Justin waited, leaning on the cement ledge, as Shania dug through her jeans' pockets.

"Here you go." Dr. Adam Raimo's cupped palm held a bank of coins.

Justin held out both hands and Adam placed the silver and copper change inside.

"Thank you," Justin said and carefully carried the coins to the ledge.

"You're welcome." Adam motioned for her to sit.

She perched, contemplating how to address her abruptness the day before as he sat beside her.

Justin moved around the fountain with shiny brass money in hand, searching for the best location to toss the coin, and then ran back to get another.

She lifted an eyebrow. "Are you stalking me?"

Adam stared into her eyes and chuckled. "No. I happened to see you and Justin as I was walking to my car."

"I see. About yesterday, I was in a rush." A new relationship wasn't on her schedule. She loved Morgan, regardless of how much it hurt. But how to tell Dr. Raimo?

"I understand. Shania..." He moved his hand to rest beside hers on the ledge.

"I want to be your friend, because I think you need someone to lean on and I want to hear your voice outside my dreams," he mumbled.

What? The last part sounded like he said he heard her voice in his dreams. Could he have been one of her clients at Companion Connections? She tried to separate out the different tones and verbiage of her clients. Most of them she'd tried to forget. "Dr. Raimo, I'm—"

"Call me Adam." He smiled.

"Adam." She laid her hands on her lap. "I need to be quite honest with you. I'm in love with someone and don't want to--"

"Shania, who do you have on your emergency contact list?"

"What?" She'd anticipated him trying to convince her to date him. Asking about her emergency call list was an odd approach.

"On your paperwork for the university, who did you put as your primary contact? I'm guessing the same person you used in Cyan." His calm voice made her nervous. Where was he going with the line of questioning?

"All of my documents have the same name listed." She wasn't going to tell him she'd put Morgan as the one. Regardless of what the future held, she could always count on him in an emergency.

"It'd take your primary contact over three hours to get here. Look, we've known each other for four years. I'd like to think we've become friends. Let me help you by being the person you call in an urgent situation." He grinned. "What better person to call than an MD, right?"

"I guess." She squinted. Possibilities and what if scenarios ran through her thoughts.

"I'm hungry. Would you and Justin like to join me for dinner? We can start to form a closer friendship, if you want."

Justin came to stand between her and Adam. What would happen to Justin if an emergency did occur? He'd be alone until Morgan arrived.

She wiggled her fingers out of Adam's grasp. "I think that's a good idea. It would be nice to have an adult to chat with for a spell. Want to go to dinner, Justin?"

He nodded. She rose and took Justin's hand into hers. "We have two hours before I go to class."

"I guess Chez Lambresko is out. We'll go to Third Generation, if Italian is okay with you?" He reached down and took Justin's free hand in his.

She glanced into Adam's eyes and down at the four hands tied together. "Yes, sounds terrific."

Shania picked up Justin and balanced him and her portfolio.

"Let me carry him." Adam reached out.

Shania met Justin's glance. He nodded. Adam took Justin, hoisting him onto his broad shoulders. Justin squealed in delight. A wild mix of emotions pulled her stomach into knots--guilt for not providing a permanent father figure and sadness the man wanting to apply for the position wasn't Morgan.

They arrived at the quaint Italian restaurant. Located downtown, the place had a lot of curb appeal. Bristol tables covered with red and white cloths strategically arranged outside under the canopies. Empty wine bottles holding unlit candles had old drops of wax hugging the sides. They made attractive tablecloth centerpieces. Later when they were lit, the ambiance would be very romantic.

"Okay if we sit outside? It's a beautiful evening." Adam glanced at her and placed Justin's feet on the brick patio.

"Sure, I don't think it'll get cold until the sun sets."

Adam asked a waiter to get them a booster seat. Shania glanced around the area. She'd been there before. Third Generation was close to a friend's old apartment. Memories came flooding back, flashes of something she didn't want to remember. She shook her head, and focused on removing Justin's backpack.

The waiter placed a plastic riser on a chair. Shania settled Justin on the square and fastened the seatbelt, hoping it'd hold him in place. She removed her bulky book-laden messenger bag and it fell to the brick floor with a thud. Adam pulled out her chair. She glanced at him, wishing he was someone else, and then lowered onto her seat.

The waiter held out a menu. She'd get something quick and enjoyable for Justin. Although she preferred unprocessed natural food, she'd let him have pizza. Adam ordered wine for himself. She asked for iced tea for herself and milk for Justin.

"What's good here?" She gave a quick glance over the menu. Garlic bread scented the air, making her stomach growl in need.

"Everything. You might like the eggplant parmesan and maybe Justin would like a pizza."

"Pizza," Justin shouted.

"Sounds delicious and the smells have me salivating already. That's what we'll have."

The waiter returned with their drinks, a basket of bread sticks and three small plates. Adam ordered their food. Other early diners arrived and took seats at nearby tables. The oak trees surrounding the restaurant held tight to their leaves instead of releasing them to organically unite with the cold soil. Still, tomato, basil and sugary dessert smells overpowered the aroma of fallen nuts.

"The weather forecaster said today would be the last warm day until next spring. We've been very lucky having the cold and snow delayed." She rambled. What nonsense was this? She'd known Adam for three plus years as Justin's pediatrician, but she didn't have a clue what to say to him as a man.

"So I hear. How are your classes going?"

Justin moved from side to side in his chair. She broke off a bit of breadstick and placed it on his plate.

Receiving crayons and a thin coloring book from the waiter, Justin squealed. Shania rejoiced in the man's opportune visit, which would hopefully prevent her son from clamoring for the contents of his backpack.

"Thank you," she said. She opened the box of crayons as he flipped through the pages.

Shania glanced at Adam. "Classes are exciting, and I'm learning so much." She reached and moved Justin's child cup to the side as the coloring book took center stage. "How about you, Adam? Are you adjusting to a different location and schedule?"

"I've been away from academics for so long I've forgotten how clever younger people can be. I swear one of my students has missed class at least six times claiming his three grandparents passed away in the last month." He touched the top of her hand as she fiddled with the red cloth napkin. "Why are you nervous?"

"What gave it away?"

"You've been on the edge of your seat since we got here. Relax, we're simply friends." He smiled and moved his hand away.

"My friend's name is Sam," Justin spouted.

"Sam's a nice name. Does he go to daycare with you?" Adam asked.

Justin nodded and picked up his breadstick.

Their food arrived and the remaining one hour and five minutes went to fast. She enjoyed the sense of family created by the evening out. Although more surprising to her was the ease of conversation between them. Adam walked them to their apartment, carrying Justin most of the way. Styrofoam containers squeaked as she held them under her arm and unlocked the door. The leftovers would provide meals for a couple of days. Justin ran inside. "Thank you for dinner, Adam."

"Would you like to go to lunch tomorrow?" He didn't try to go inside, and Shania appreciated his consideration.

"I have a class at noon." She fought the urge to step away, to put distance between them. Her palms flooded with moisture. If he made a romantic gesture, she'd have to act. One step and she was on the other side of the threshold. Justin stepped into the bathroom. She could escape an awkward end to the pseudo-date by declaring she needed to help him. As she opened her mouth to say the words, the toilet flushed and a few minutes later the television came on.

"Then for dinner tomorrow night or Saturday." He smiled, revealing bright white teeth. The shimmer of laughter in his eyes indicated he'd noticed her retreat.

"Justin and I could go out tomorrow night, but I have to study this weekend. I have a project due in my drawing class."

He frowned. The invitation probably wasn't for both of them, but she wasn't going alone on a date with him.

"Great. I'll pick you both up at six?"

She nodded. "Good night, Adam."

"Until tomorrow, Shania," he softly replied and leaned in. She thought he was going to kiss her. Instead he pulled the door shut.

* * * *

Justin fell asleep following one story of Diego's explorations and two choruses of *Good Night, Sleep Tight*. Shania sat in the groove of the cushions of the sofa, pressing her fingers into the expanding hole. Soon it would be the size of a quarter. She tugged the thin azure threads trying to cover the padding underneath. Should she call? Weighing the pros and cons of a phone call to her friend, Shania might find out what was happening in Cyan or that they'd moved on and didn't miss her. A risk, but one she'd take.

Before she could change her mind her index finger pressed the quick connect button, eight on her cellphone tying her to her past.

"Companion Connections, this is Liz." The breathy smoker's voice, bigger than life, filled the phone. Tears instantly formed in Shania's eyes. Liz was family. Shania missed her almost as much as Morgan.

"Hi, Liz, it's Shay." She sounded breathy. Shania's work ID was Shay Lei. Whenever they were at the office they always addressed each other by their caller name to make it inherent to their jobs. Shania wove her fingers through her hair. Why was she anxious?

"Girl, where have you been? You said you'd stay in touch. I've been worried! The ladies and I came to get you to celebrate. Your place was empty. Now, I understand you wanted to quit the job, but I hadn't realized you wanted to quit Cyan." Her voice rolled out with anger and fear. Underlying both was love.

Shania drew in a breath and wiped a tear from her cheek. "Liz, I'm sorry I didn't tell you. I needed to break free."

"Are you safe?"

"Yes. We're getting comfortable."

"Are you happy, Shay?"

She could imagine a stern expression on Liz's beautiful round face. Shania sniffed. She gripped a loose thread between her fingers and tore one of the thin strands from the sofa. The quarter size hole would grow if she kept tugging the strings. "Yes, I'm doing what I've wanted to do for a long time."

"I'm not going to ask where you're at, because I understand about starting over, honey. We've all started over here at Companion Connections. Call me as often as you're able and if you need anything, I'm here for you." She breathed into the phone. Daughtry sang *Over You* in the background.

The lyrics were so true--"build me up and tear me down." That's what she thought of Morgan. He created a world of love and security and then...

"Thanks, Liz. I feel better knowing I have family like you."

"Now you've got me bawling like that little baby of yours. How is he?" Liz's voice sounded raspy, raspier than normal, and she sniffed.

"He's good, growing like a weed. What are you celebrating?" Shania sprinkled a happy tune in her tone.

"One of the bosses dumped his girlfriend. We're all excited, 'cause she was nothing but trouble. Although it happened a few months ago, this is the first night most of us could get together. You know how it is, working nights, it's hit and miss." The last word was muted, as if she'd placed her hand over the receiver. "Sorry. Belle put on some funky music."

"Cool." Shania smiled. Pleasant memories of getting together with some of the other callers during the day came to mind. She'd enjoyed becoming friends with her co-workers and especially some of her older clients. Lonesome people seeking companionship, someone to talk with.

"Shay, I've a final check for you. What do you want me to do with it?"

"Could you hold it, and I'll come by over Christmas break?" Shania didn't want her new address to be given to anyone at her home town. She wanted no contact with any of her family members, if they were inclined. "Sure. How are classes going?" Clever Liz, she'd no doubt figured out why Shania left. Of course, during the monthly staff meetings, Shania always had a book or sketch pad in hand. Her mentor used logical reasoning. Shania hoped to be like Liz in the future, independent and sassy.

"Good. I'm doing what I've always wanted to do, learn about art."

"Are you ready to come back? Before you start making excuses, it's a telephone connection so you don't need to be nearby and your clients miss you." She coughed. "We miss you."

"Are you crying? Don't cry for me, Liz." Shania wiped her own eyes.

"I remember when you first came to see me about the job, pregnant and nineteen years old. A baby having a baby." Sniffles rang through the phone.

"Do you really want to go down memory lane when you have a dynamite party to attend? I can hear a song by Flo Rida coming through the phone." Shania didn't want to shake off that part of her life. The job benefited her in more than supplying her with funds, she'd gained friends. As a result of talking--rather listening--to lonely people discuss their past mistakes, she'd learned, grown, and matured. The move forced both her and Justin to become more independent. They would get past the new and frightening routines.

"I'll always have time for you, Shay." Liz sighed. "How is Justin doing?"

"He has ups and downs. Daycare is good for him, but he resents being away from me." She had a visual of meeting Liz at a coffee shop to be interviewed for the job of companion. An information flyer detailing the position of connections representative had arrived in her mailbox just as her funds ran out.

"If I can't convince you to come back to work, will you at least promise to call now and again?"

"Yes, I will. Liz, I'm tired of being alone. I understand how our clients feel." She hadn't tried to disguise the melancholy in her voice.

"Oh, Shay, you told the guy you loved him," she whispered as the husky-hued musician sang about going home.

"Yes, but my timing wasn't perfect. I should have listened to your suggestions sooner." She bit her lip, rubbing her teeth back and forth across the surface.

"What happened?"

Shania tried to lose the tears forming, but the memory of when she should have told Morgan her true feelings came rushing through her mind. Why hadn't she told him before, when she'd trapped him in the closet?

"I called him to my house to get rid of a creature above the broom closet. I heard clawing and chewing."

"Good location to tell someone you love them, trapped in a small space." The squeak of a chair came over the phone line. "Shay, could you hold for a moment? I've got another call coming in?"

"Sure." Just talking about the day Shania wanted to tell Morgan she loved him brought her happy and sad feelings. She remembered their conversation as if it happened yesterday instead of several months ago.

Morgan had arrived to help her set traps to get rid of a mouse climbing through the rafters. Shania scraped her fingernails along the white woodwork near the door in the kitchen, imitating the sound a rodent would make. He immediately stopped her fingers from scratching the wall. Her intention was to make the noise annoying so he'd understand how much it bothered her.

He gave her a quirky grin and opened the closet door.

"Go inside or you won't hear anything." Lips suddenly dry, Shania swiped her tongue to lubricate them.

He stared at her and groused, "Both of us won't fit."

She touched his chest to feel his deep breaths and heart pounding. "Gosh, I didn't realize you were an asthmatic, or do you have a phobia of closets?"

"The space is too tight."

Shania grimaced at his response. "Then am I to assume you believe my rear is too big?' Placing her hands on her behind, she desperately wanted to look in a mirror.

"No such luck," he wheezed.

She twisted trying to get a view. "I know my butt is larger than before I had Justin. Do you think it's massive?"

Instead of replying he said, "Burrs. Thick pointed thistles, don't go near them."

"What?" Shania asked.

"I can help you with this problem, *Shania.*" He hit her name hard as if he was angry.

Ready to give up the idea of telling him of her love, she pressed closer. She had to get near the door and leave the tiny room.

"Shh. Listen. Do you hear the noise?" There wasn't scratching. She only heard the gas heater humming in the background.

Shania held still, her hand flush against his heaving chest. She couldn't hear anything over their breathing.

She inhaled, bringing in the scent of his cologne, bergamot and citrus. "I don't hear anything."

He blew out a breath. "Please be quiet."

She closed her eyes, remembering his gentle caressing touch. She had leaned into him, moved her arm up around his neck and relaxed. More than catching the creature, she wanted a kiss from him. He was breathing like he'd run a marathon.

The click of a line reconnecting brought Shania out of her remembrance.

"Sorry, Shay, that was a tangled issue. You were telling me how you wanted to tell your guy that you loved him by trapping him in a closet."

"Yeah, it didn't work. He started huffing air as if he was claustrophobic."

"So, you didn't tell him you love him because you care so much?" Liz's question brought Shania firmly back to the present.

Shania's gut clenched in agony. His closeness had been pleasure and pain. "Yes."

"So you never got the words out?"

"No, just as well, maybe we weren't meant to be together. I've learned from the past, love hurts." She took a deep breath. "I tried to talk to him several times. Six months ago when I went to his house, he was otherwise occupied. The next time I went to him, alone and ready to talk, he was rushing to his parents' place for a celebration. I thought I had a chance to reveal my feelings as he was leaving for his bachelor party but that didn't work. Finally, I was able to dance with him during the rehearsal dinner, but--"

"Oh, no, don't tell me," Liz snickered.

"Yes, right before the wedding I had a full minute to talk to him."

"Oh, Shay. How risky." She paused. "The ceremony was about two months ago?"

"Yes, and I can't get him out of my system." Shania swallowed, grabbed her blouse, and massaged her chest trying to relieve the ache.

"What happened?"

"I said 'I love you.' His bride-to-be overheard and tossed me out."

"Oh dear, did he call?" Her voice was angry and elated at the same time. The odd mix of emotions filtered through the connection.

"I saw him later that night. He didn't say if he was married or not. He left and I haven't heard from him. Maybe I read the signs wrong."

"No, dear, you didn't read the signs wrong. He's into you. You. I'm not sure why he didn't chase you down." "Bastard" might have been voiced under Liz's breath. The party was becoming louder.

"Don't worry, Liz. Maybe my timing threw him into a tailspin or perhaps he truly loves her." Shania pressed an index finger between her breasts. The pain now blocked her throat.

"I don't think so." Liz hummed along with the muffled music. "Listen, Shay, I want you to kiss that boy for me and call again. I'll hold your check for you. Let me know in advance when you're coming, and we'll go to lunch or dinner. Okay?"

"Thanks, Liz. It's good to hear your voice." Shania didn't want the call to end, but she'd kept Liz away from her celebration long enough. "I'll call in December."

"Thanks, hun, and Shay...don't worry, it'll all work out in your favor. Have faith in love."

Chapter 5

Morgan glanced through the office building window. Liz, beaming as if she'd won the lottery, walked out of her office and wiggled her way into the center of a cluster of girls.

He didn't know their names. They must work at Companion Connections because the locked entry into the building required fingerprint identification and keycard. High security was a method of keeping clients out and maintaining a protected environment for the staff and records. Wish he'd thought of it. Instead his partner, Tom, had. Bottom line was the employees would be safe.

They were perfectly protected except the heavy metal door shut too slowly. Morgan slid in after a dark-haired beauty. Once he finished riffling through the records, he'd give Tom a call and advise him of the problem. Anyone could slip inside and their business would be subject to robbery or worse.

As Morgan walked through the open space, he glanced at the female gaggle, a colorful arrangement of white, black, red and golden goddesses. The women were dressed in a variety of apparel from sleek, sparkly, short skirts to jeans. Their body shapes varied from tall and thin to short and stocky. The only common denominators were their sunny personalities and sexy voices. He'd entered a room full of husky-timbered Leona Lewises and Kathleen Turners--or even Lana Turners, as some of the companions had to be as old as black and white movies. The one he wanted wasn't a part of the group.

The beautiful flock waved at him. Music with a snappy beat vibrated his eardrums. Lyrics depicting doing it on the floor made him question their music choice. Obviously not bothering the women as they concentrated on their dancing, chatting and drinking. A simple sofa and two club chairs had been pushed to the side. He slipped into the office Liz had exited from and softly shut the door. The click could not be heard over the shouting, laughing, and singing along with the song. He glanced out the office window. There wasn't a banner declaring what they were celebrating. Regardless, the ladies were having a good time.

Morgan walked into the classic office--beige walls, black iron lamps on the tables at the ends of a brown suede sofa and a large antique desk directly in the middle of the room. The space was dark. He itched to turn on one of the lamps. He didn't dare. She'd catch him and drop-kick him out the door. Behind the desk chair was a set of file cabinets. Would they be unlocked? He slid his finger into the metal handle and tugged.

The drawer snicked open. Sweet success. He pulled it enough to catch some light from the hallway outside and riffled through the folders until he came across the name he'd been searching. Shay Lei AKA Shania Miller. He glanced out the window to find the motley crew line dancing. Some of the women were on top of the tables and others straddled chairs. He tried to listen to the current song, but didn't recognize the artist nor understand the words. Liz continued to shake her generous booty.

The heavy steel office door provided the privacy needed to conduct business. Morgan glanced at the documents in his hand and lifted the corners with two fingers. Should he invade her records? What would he see? As Shania's indirect boss, he had the right to review her work records. So why did he feel like he was betraying a trust?

He took a deep relaxing breath. His goal was only to find out her address. That was it. His gaze shot out the window. Fuck. Liz was making her way to the office. He'd been spotted. Morgan slipped the folder back into the cabinet, uncaring where it was placed. He skidded around the desk and landed onto the seat of a leather chair. He took a deep breath and slowly exhaled. Liz flipped on the light switch. The bright glow illuminated the room.

"What are you doing in here?" Liz's croaky voice held a snippet of anger mixed with a chuckle. Was the laughter a carry-over from the party or directed at him?

He disregarded her question. "What's going on out there?"

"We're celebrating," she quipped.

He smiled. Liz was worth every penny he paid. He admired her dedication to the job. She was the best manager he'd ever hired, but her sense of humor was what he valued the most.

Liz glanced at the file cabinet and then at him. Morgan had the strongest urge to squirm in his seat. No fingerprints were on the metal. Nothing had been shifted on top. Her office chair was in perfect alignment with the desk, yet she knew.

"Do you have psychic powers, Miz Liz?" he asked and flashed a grin. From the time he was the tender age of two his "sweet little smile" had always gotten him out of trouble. Would his luck hold?

"You betcha, so what are you trying to find in the files, young man?" She plopped onto the chair. Resting elbows on the desk, she folded her hands together and propped her chin on top.

"Liz, Liz, Liz." He flashed the grin again. The clever woman seemed to know everything. He should have anticipated getting caught and formed a plausible excuse.

"The truth shall set you free," she pronounced, her stare intense and pious.

He blinked.

She smiled and shifted her hands to rest on top of the desk. Her shiny mouth curved slightly at the corners.

"I want a forwarding address for one of your girls," he admitted and licked his very dry lips.

"First off, they are not girls. They are women who are employed to provide comfort and conversation to companionless people." She narrowed her eyes and her fingernails dug into the desk blotter. "Our business, if you'll recollect, is called Companion Connections."

"I know that, Liz. I'm sorry for the wrong terminology. Typical of me to piss off my best friend." He grinned and reached forward to touch her hand.

Her brown-eyed gaze softened at the same time her fingers entwined with his. "Mmm-hmm, friends."

"Ah, Liz, if only I was free. I'd be all over your sexy woman body." He sighed. She blushed, adding bright red from her cheekbones down along her neck. Her broad smile narrowed.

"You devil. I never know when to believe you. You canceled your wedding with Petulant Patty."

"Don't call her that," Morgan said. "You were there, so you know I ended it." This wasn't going well.

"Right. Now you're riffling through my files, looking for an address." She released his hand and smoothed down her salt and pepper hair. Her fingers clasped the deep V of her fuchsia dress and tugged it, drawing his attention to her chest and the brilliant diamond on a very important finger. "Who does your heart belong to, then?"

"New ring? You're kidding me?" He sat against the backrest and laughed. "You're getting married? You?"

"Hey, even the unbelievable and uncompromising can be convinced to love. Devon is a wonderful man. I'm lucky...er... He's lucky to have found me." She held her age-spotted hand in front of her, the diamonds glittering in the overhead light.

Morgan laughed louder, and then lowered his eyelids halfway. "I guess I didn't act fast enough to catch you, Liz. Do I have time to make a play for you?"

"You fiend. You're only saying that because you know once I commit it's a forever thing. Stop trying to change the subject. I'm not going to leave you alone in here, so get over the idea of riffling through the files. Just tell me who has caught your eye."

"My love. She put knots in my heartstrings from the day I met her." He sobered and propped his ankle on his knee.

"Oh? Heartstrings? Interesting." She leaned forward and pierced him with a look, an intense stare. "We've been friends for what, ten years now? You need to divulge all of your secrets. I think I already know why you were nosing around in my folders. So tell."

Morgan cleared his throat. Should he confess to Liz? He'd always kept his personal life and professional business separate. However, Shania had called and when he rang back there wasn't a connection. She could be in danger. According to Tom, Beck was showing signs of erratic anger. Pain in his chest prevented him from breathing normally. What if something had happened to her? He'd never told her that he loved her.

"Shay. I'm in love with Shania Miller. She moved away from Cyan, and I can't locate her. Tell me where she's gone?" He lowered his leg, leaned forward and placed his hand on the desk. Ready to grab a pen and paper if needed to write down details. As if necessary, he scoffed. He'd find out the address, commit it to memory, and then he'd go get her.

"No." She puffed out a long breath. The scent of whisky floated in the space around him.

"What?" He shook his head. His listening skills needed to improve.

"I don't know her address. She called earlier tonight. I'm holding a paycheck for her until December." Liz hadn't blinked. Her body movements were straight, unmoving. She was telling the truth. "She's fine, Morgan."

Chapter 6

"Miss Miller, please stay a moment after class." Monsieur Barrett hovered beside her easel, glancing at her work instead of into her eyes. Her breakfast toast spoiled in her stomach. Background noises--students packing away their supplies, stuffing portfolios or backpacks and exiting--didn't distract her from the demand.

Shania glanced at Justin who was dragging a miniature truck across the tiled floor of the professor's office. The first hour of class her son quietly drew on his artist pad. For the last thirty minutes he'd made motor sounds. He wasn't disruptive. She didn't think his murmurings bothered anyone. Sharp angry looks didn't get shot his way, nor had anyone asked about him.

Monsieur Barrett wandered into his office once, talked to Justin for a couple of minutes and came out again. He'd had a smile on his face. Had her son later destroyed something? She stowed her work in progress in her cubicle and wiped the charcoal from her fingers. Hoisting her bag, she made her way into the room.

She sat on the hard chair opposite the professor's desk. Justin climbed onto her lap, truck in hand.

"Your son used my charcoals while I was teaching." He grabbed Justin's small artist pad and placed it on the desk.

"I'm sorry, sir. I'll replace the pencils." She held Justin close. "He's never used something that wasn't his without permission before."

"The reason I'm mentioning it is because of what he did with the charcoals." He reached across the desk.

"I'm sorry, sir. He's three, and although he tries to stay in the lines, sometimes misses happen." Cripes, how much would she have to pay to replace the ruined item? She mentally waved goodbye to their winter coats as she looked around the room, trying to find what had been damaged.

"He's three?" he asked as he lifted the cover of the pad.

"Yes, sir. He'll be four at the end of April." Because of his young age would the professor forgive and forget? In her mind she envisioned the winter coats back into her closet with new department store tags hanging from the cuffs.

"You claimed he was a good child and you were right. He resembles his father in more than appearance." He flipped a few pages of crayon renditions, and then turned the page around so she could see the charcoal drawing.

She gasped. "Oh, my."

"'Oh, my' is right, Miss Miller. Your son is a genius. He obviously listened to the lecture today and, unlike a few of your colleagues, applied the information." Monsieur Barrett gently removed the page and held it up. "This is a perfect example of Gainsborough's unconventional chalk on gray cotton style. See how the books and papers have feathery surface patterns and the lone truck sits on top? The sketch has rhythmic layers. The chalk strokes are diagonal emphasizing the focal point. Justin, did you draw this picture?"

Justin nodded.

"Do you mind if I try to get this piece into an art show?" Monsieur Barrett laid the drawing on the credenza behind him. Was he so sure of her answer?

Excitement jetted through her. Her three-year-old son might have his work in an art show. "Yes!"

"No. For Mommy." Justin scooted off her lap, shook off her hand and scuttled to his drawing.

"Honey, why don't we let Monsieur Barrett show other people your beautiful picture? I bet he'll frame the art for you, and when he's done we'll hang it at home." She glanced at her professor, who smiled and nodded.

"By the TV?" Justin asked. She chuckled inside. Behind the television was prime real estate. They'd been looking for the perfect piece for the wall since they'd moved to Briarwood.

"Yes, I think that would be the ideal location." She grinned at her clever son.

Justin smiled and switched his attention to Monsieur. "Okay."

"I want him to try still-life next week."

"What? I don't think so," she hissed. "The still-life scheduled is a nude."

"No, not a model. Fruit or flowers. Simple. Not a lot of detail, a single flower or an apple." He muttered and flipped through his old-fashioned rolodex. "You'll show him some of the Clara Peters, or as you'd prefer impressionist point to a Van Gogh and Cezanne in your text?"

"Yes, I'll show him." She wanted to shout her joy, exclaim to everyone of her young son's amazing ability.

"I'll expect you to bring him next week then." Monsieur Barrett rubbed his hands together. Was his enthusiasm only for Justin, or due to the fact her child's talent was more remarkable than Beck's? Beck Longview had a charcoal currently hanging in the university's art museum. During a weak moment she took Justin to see Beck's art. She didn't tell her son the sketch had been created by his biological father.

"Yes, sir." She repacked Justin's trucks and helped him into his jacket. Her bag firmly set on her back, she took her talented son's hand and they left the building. A block later she sat on the edge of the fountain, dug into her jeans pocket, and drew out coins. She handed them to Justin. Pleased he didn't have to ask, he took the bits of brass.

"Don't forget to make a wish."

He tossed the coins into the fountain with exuberance and a concentrated expression. Shania removed her cellphone and pressed the number two button. Morgan should be the first to know.

The phone rang four times when a female voice came on instructing the caller to leave a message after the tone. She snapped the cell closed, cutting off the connection. She needed to share her elation with him. Justin's first word was voiced in front of both of them. Justin took his first steps to reach his surrogate father. Morgan taught him how to use the big boy toilet. He was always the first to hear good news.

She rubbed her head in misery. Morgan had been a part of their lives for the past four years and now he wasn't. He didn't know where to find them. She had left Cyan and traveled to Briarwood without telling him. No note. No call. No last good-bye.

"Deception and truth eventually coincide," she said to herself. Justin glanced at her and continued to play. She should have made an effort to tell Morgan how she felt. Shania had the perfect opportunity the day of the rodent incident. Who was she kidding? There were several occasions she'd lost or ignored. She'd missed Morgan every minute of every day since they'd arrived in Briarwood. He was her primary contact and her heart bled thinking he wouldn't be any longer. Why hadn't he called her? Normally, he would have, regardless of the incident in the church. He'd given her mixed messages by coming to see her and asking if she meant what she'd said and then left. Had Morgan given up on them?

"Mommy, why are you crying?" Justin snuggled beside her.

"I'm happy. You're a very good artist, honey." She wiped her face with the sleeves of her sweater. "Come on, we'll go get ready for our dinner with Dr. Raimo."

"Okay. Look, there's Megan." Justin pointed to his Thursday night babysitter. "Hi Megan," he shouted and waved.

The perky black-haired teen, a piercing through her left eyebrow and another four on each ear, jogged up to them. Her black sweat pants, rolled to her knees, displayed a colorful butterfly on her ankle. She wore a matching zippered jacket with a dragon on the right shoulder.

"There's my favorite kid in the whole world." Megan leaned down and hugged him.

Justin wiggled free, but stayed close.

"Hey, Shania, what's happening?" She sat on the edge of the fountain and smoothed her fingers through Justin's blond hair.

"Same ol', same ol'." Shania didn't want to tell anyone else about the possible art show in case it fell through. "Would you be able to cut my hair today?"

She would shed her exterior and create a new stronger woman. Someone who didn't need a man to feel secure, successful. She and Justin would make their own way in spite of the odds.

"Sure. Are you talking a trim?" She lifted a lock of Shania's hair. Justin ran to the edge of the grass. His toes touched the green, while his heels remained solid on the cement. He wanted to run, but he wouldn't.

"No, I want something new. Contemporary. Easy care."

"Great, I have something in mind. Can I cut the kid's hair too? His shag's long enough to braid," Megan said. Shania glanced at Justin who caught a ball and tossed it toward a dog. He shook the hair from his eyes. Blocked vision wasn't good. Why hadn't she noticed?

"Yes, but I can't pay you until next week, is that okay?" The extra twenty from daycare would be spent, but they both needed a fresh look, and she wanted help with a new attitude.

"Great, let's go." Megan ran to Justin, grabbed him around the waist, and swung him around.

Shania picked up Justin's backpack and slid the tiny strap on one shoulder. As the trio made their way to Shania's apartment, her stomach roiled. She would hide the bruised side of her core, and prevent further pain and injury. An uncomplicated solution to take the anguish away would be to start with a make-over.

What seemed like hours later she glanced in the bathroom mirror, not believing how much her appearance had changed with a simple haircut.

Her head felt lighter. She tilted her face to the side. The bob scarcely moved as her head turned. Combed down the center instead of on one side, bangs drew attention to her almond shaped eyes. She glanced at Justin, who was watching cartoons. Bob the Builder was searching for treasure with a friendly cowgirl. Justin's fine hair cropped close to his head made him look like a little boy instead of her baby.

Megan, quite pleased with her work, had danced away when her mother called her to dinner.

Shania's axis had shifted from stay-at-home-Mom to a full-time-student—and a woman whose love for a man wasn't returned. She needed to speed forward and let the past remain in Cyan. Did she want to readjust? Love for Morgan would not become history. Her stomach hurt at night as she lay in bed watching the gargoyle on the windowsill. Awake, she contemplated the future and it looked bleak without the real Morgan.

Her cellphone rang. She pulled the mobile connection from its purse pocket. As she opened the top, a low battery message slid across the face. The phone immediately shut down. She took the device into the bedroom and connected it to the charger.

Ring-ling sounded through the small apartment. She hurried to the door and opened to reveal a very hunky man. Her eyes scanned the tip of his shiny black shoes to his neatly pressed slacks, snug fitting jacket, crisp white shirt and plain red tie. Adam in a suit was gorgeous. His dark eyes glimmered with humor, as if he knew where her thoughts took her.

"Hi, Shania. Your hair is very pretty like that." He swirled his finger in the air, drawing an invisible line around her face.

"Thank you. You look great."

"Ditto. Ready to go?" His smile brightened his face.

"Sure, let me get my wrap. Justin, are you ready?" She took Justin's coat from the rack and laid it on the back of the sofa.

"Can I take my truck?" he shouted from the bedroom.

"One Matchbox. Come on." She tucked her arms into the black cashmere woven cloak, a cast-off from her mother years before. Adam held the garment steady.

Justin ran out of the bedroom stuffing a tiny short-bed truck into his pocket. "Ready."

She held out his coat and shoved his arms through the sleeves. As they took the two steps to the door she remembered her phone. "Oh, wait. I need to get my cellphone."

Shania ran to the bedroom and unplugged the phone. The face didn't light up. Crap, she couldn't afford a new cell. Maybe the thing still worked. As she walked into the living room, she pressed buttons and the call rang through to Megan.

"What's wrong?" Adam asked.

"Nothing, it's just my phone face went out. No lights behind it." She shoved the deep blue rectangle into her square purse.

"Do you want me to take a look at it?" Adam asked.

She quirked a brow. "Do you know a lot about phones?"

"No, but I'm familiar with antiques and that looks like an antique." He grinned and lifted the car seat beside the door.

"Ha, ha. Let's go. I'm hungry." Shania slipped the strap of her purse over her arm and walked through the exit. Justin followed and grabbed her hand.

Adam secured the child's seat into the back of his red Volvo and strapped Justin in. "Do you like Japanese?" he asked as he slid behind the wheel.

"Sure, we both do. What restaurant, Ching's or Jo-Do's?"

"Jo-Do's okay with you?" He started the car and glanced at her.

"Yes. Fantastic." She smiled. He grinned in response.

Jo-Do's wait-staff dressed in authentic white kosode robes and *hakama*. The comfortable looking garments consisted of a simple pattern of rectangles. She loved relaxed clothing. Adam carried Justin. They were shown to a table near the windows overlooking a Zen garden.

Once seated, she tried to instruct Justin in the art of using chopsticks as Adam ordered a family meal. The food arrived, starting with egg drop soup. To Shania's surprise, Justin consumed most of the broth. He created a ramp with the wooden utensils, then drove his truck up and down.

"Tell me about your family, Adam," Shania asked and shifted the partially filled bowls to the edge of the table and out of the line of a falling toy.

"My parents live five miles outside of Briarwood. My father taught physics here at BU, my mother's a doctor. It seemed natural for me to do both." He took a sip of his Saki and shifted his chair.

He'd unbound his neck tie. It hung an inch from his throat. The top button was unfastened and dark curls of hair sprung through the opening. His Adam's apple worked up and down as he talked.

He placed the glass on the table. "I have two brothers and three sisters. All of them are married and have a horde of kids. I enjoy watching football, basketball, baseball and hockey. You could say I enjoy sports. However, I only played tennis, soccer and baseball in high school. House hunting is taking up a lot of my time."

She took a sip of her water, placed the glass on the table and asked, "Where are you looking for a house? Near your parents?"

"Near the university. I teach night class, so it's easier to be close to work." He pressed his back against the chair so the waiter could place dishes in front of them. "I like the older stately houses near your complex."

"Favorite color?"

"Red." He speared his fish.

"Favorite musical artist?" She took a bite of her veggie noodle dish.

"For each genre?"

"Ah, I guess I'll find out through experience. I'm assuming Rascal Flatts is your country fave since we listened to the Flatts' recent CD on the way to the restaurant?" she asked.

"I have to go potty," Justin announced.

"Let's go." Shania placed her napkin beside her plate, hoisted her purse over her shoulder and shoved her chair away from the table. Adam stood. She walked around to lift Justin off his booster seat. "Excuse us. We'll be right back."

Several moments later they returned. Adam stood and pulled out Justin's chair and then hers. She strapped Justin in and took her seat.

"Thank you." She placed the napkin on her lap. "I've delayed your dinner enough, let's eat."

He touched her arm. "I kind of thought you'd ditch me."

"Why? I'm having a good time, talking and becoming friends. Aren't you?" She moved food around on her plate. Adam was nice. She hoped they could be more than acquaintances. Her heart skipped a beat as she thought of Morgan. Bruised spirit or not, she couldn't easily get over him. Her love remained true.

"Yes, I am. How about dinner on Tuesday?" He lowered his hand and picked up his fork.

"Sounds lovely." She took a bite of carrot. The sharp scent of the vegetable infiltrated her senses.

"And next Sunday? It's my mother's birthday. If I don't take a date, she'll set me up with every available female in Briarwood. Would you go with me as my friend-date?" His eyes glowed and held a smidgen of his previous success.

Smooth. He maneuvered her by confirming they were friends, got her sympathy by stating it was a celebration for his mother, and ended with save-me-she'll-make-me-date-her-women-choices. She felt conflicted. Too much, too fast, three friend dates in one week was a lot. She'd make the excuse of no babysitter.

"They love kids. My mother's anxious to meet Justin. I've talked about him quite a bit." Adam finished his meal and scooted the dish away.

"What did you say?" Justin asked.

Adam laughed. "That you were adorable, smart and you liked trucks."

"I like trucks." He yawned.

"Let's see how Tuesday goes first." She placed her napkin on the table. Her cold food grew undesirable. Their friendship had quickly gone from occasional get-togethers for coffee to scheduled events. "Ready to go home, Justin?"

"Uh-huh."

Adam graciously paid the bill, settled them into his Volvo sedan, and after a short drive they arrived at her apartment. He carried a sleeping Justin, child seat and all, to the door. As a friend, he was very considerate and very strong. Maybe their friendship would work out. Perhaps she misjudged his motives. She resented the bit of arrogance in herself, thinking he wanted to date her.

"Thank you, Adam, for dinner. I had a lovely time," she quietly said. She unlocked the door and took Justin from him.

He leaned and kissed the side of her face. His lips were dry, but his thoughtfulness was nice. "So did I. Tuesday at six."

"Good night," she whispered. She set the booster seat down in the living room. The click of the door as it shut furthered her thoughts of his kindness.

As she lifted Justin out of his seat, her cellphone rang for the first time that night. She carried him to bed and removed his clothing. By the time she got her purse open the ringing stopped. The face was dark. The phone had finally died a silent cold death.

Chapter 7

"Dad?" Morgan entered his parents' home through the kitchen door. A bell attached at the top of the window pane jingled. The chime was a recent addition. His father had installed the signal so Morgan's mother, Margaret, could hear when someone entered the house. The Hardwick homestead was situated in a wooded lot half-a-mile from Country Road 200, two miles in front of the veterinary clinic. Sometimes desperate animal owners chose to come to the house instead of driving back to the brick building. Often they'd enter without knocking or ringing the bell, and had scared the hell out of his mother on occasion.

His father, Mark, had become quiet this past year. Steady in his work ethic, he didn't veer from his routine. He had a firm philosophy: Work starts at sunrise and ends at sunset. A person should always keep his or her debts at a minimum. If a person doesn't have cash they shouldn't buy it. Mark was to retire next month. Perhaps his silence related to the impending departure from his practice. Accustomed to a full day of activity, he was having difficulty adjusting to retirement.

"I'm watching the Pacers, Morgan," his father shouted from two rooms over.

Morgan's ancestral home was decorated in American Traditional. His mother claimed the Patriotic American knicknacks were not clutter. Morgan didn't allege to be a decorator, but it sure looked like hodgepodge to him. His mom loved to accumulate anything from American Flags folk art to those baskets--Longaberger or something. He admitted he'd added to the masses by creating pieces of furniture for her to store her collectibles. His father groaned as Mother's Day came around, knowing another handcrafted unit to hold her stuff would be coming into the house.

The hallway wall was nearly filled with more of her breakables. He glanced at a new oil painting depicting typical simple Amish life. A woman raked a hoe through a vegetable garden. In the background, a boy child held a wood plank swing, ready to release a tiny girl holding onto thick ropes tied to a fat-branched oak tree. Morgan focused on his mission. His father reclined in a mustard-colored leather chair watching the basketball game. His gray-haired mother sat on the sofa to the right of his father's easy-chair, cross-stitching near a bright table lamp. Her long slender fingers, still nimble, weaved the thread in and out of the cloth. The clink of her ring bumping against the wooden bracket chimed through the room.

"Hey, where have you been the last couple of months?" His father muted the sound on the television. The sprinkling of silver had taken over, leaving only a small amount of visible blond. Noticeable excess rested on his belt line, a result of attending meals on a regular basis.

"Busy. Are the ladies still bringing their pets in for check-ups so they can look over the new partner? What did the office staff call the guy? Some odd term."

"Hunk-a-V," his mother supplied.

Mark snorted. "Waning."

Morgan tried to smile. He was about to reveal something he wasn't proud of, yet he knew they would always be there for him and trust they'd be fair and honest. If he needed a good shaking, they'd give it. He coughed, trying to open his closed throat. "I need to ask for your help."

His mother put her stitching on the coffee table. "Sit, I'll get you a glass of water."

"Thanks, Mom." He sat on the edge of the sofa, still anxious. His chest eased a little knowing he wasn't alone. Unfortunately, his mind created different violent scenarios in his head of Shania and Justin being held hostage or killed.

His mother hustled into the room and handed him the glass. He sipped. The cold fluid slid down his throat. It tasted delicious, so he drank the remainder.

His father switched off the basketball game.

"Shania and Justin left town, and I can't locate them. I went to the house the day after the canceled wedding and it was empty. Her neighbors refused to give me information. Her mail's not being forwarded."

"That poor girl. Something horrible must have happened to make her leave. She loved living in your small house." His mother touched his arm. "It seems like yesterday instead of four years ago you brought her to us. Poor girl, heartbroken and pregnant... It's hard to believe she'd leave without telling you."

"I know she loved the house." But did she love him? "I'm shocked she left without a word."

She picked up her stitching. "She's such a sweet girl. When it was obvious Beck didn't want to be with her, I imagined you two would get together. Maybe she couldn't reach you because you weren't answering your phone. I've tried to call and a monotone female recording told me you weren't available."

His father leaned on the arm of the chair.

Morgan bit the inside of his cheek. He didn't want to burden his parents with his mistakes. They'd taught him better. "I love Shania."

There, easy enough.

"Son, we've known that since you first met the girl. When she stayed with us, we came to care for her. She's a lovely young woman, sweet, honest, proud and a hard worker. The horses loved her, and they are always a judge of good character." His father tapped his finger on the chair arm. "You didn't tell us exactly what happened at the church. We thought it was your business. Considering this--" He waved his hand at Morgan. "--Shania must have been involved. Do you want to share with us now?"

Morgan couldn't get past the character and horse reference. Had she helped with the drafts? Their massive hoofs would have crushed her. He'd ask for details later. "Shania came to me in the chancery. She said she loved me."

"And?" his father prompted.

"Let's just say Patty was rude. I broke the engagement. As you know I canceled the ceremony, and I'm almost finished paying for my half of the wedding. I'm probably paying for all of it." He glanced at his watch, needing to get to his night construction job soon.

"Do you want me to talk to her mother?" Maggie glanced over the top of her eyeglasses.

Morgan held the laughter inside. Was it his mom or were all women under the illogical belief they could solve problems by talking mother to mother? "No, thank you, Mom. Another week of working nights and I'll be finished. Tell me how to find Shania? I'm scared she needs help. When I call her cellphone, I keep getting an out of service message."

"Have you talked to her friends?" His mother propped her glasses on top of her head.

"Yes, during the past few weeks I've checked with as many as possible." Morgan rubbed his chest. An ache had been present since she walked out of the church. He should have told her he loved her that night. However, it seemed wrong to walk away from a wedding and a couple of hours later tell another woman of his feelings for her. Would she have believed him? He'd wanted her to see him as a desirable man for such a long time. He'd convinced himself her declaration of love hadn't occurred. What if she had said "Patty doesn't love you," and in his mind he'd heard "I love you"? If he had been thinking clearly, he would have known before the wedding incident that Patty wanted to be married and anyone would suffice. Morgan had needed an escape from his fantasies, his longing, to be with Shania.

"Go to her parents." His father picked up the remote.

"Why would you think they'd know where she'd be? Remember I brought her here after her folks abandoned her and Beck's parents refused to believe her." Morgan didn't trust the Millers or the Longviews.

"Morgan, don't give me that look. I remember exactly how distraught Shania was and the bits of conversation she replayed. Her parents kept track of her. Back in early summer, I was at Shania's house fixing the water heater when I witnessed Mrs. Miller driving by. She turned her head quick enough, but I glimpsed her face," Mark said.

"And my hairdresser knows Anne's stylist, they go to the same conferences. Did you know hairdressers go to shows and conventions?"

"Maggie," his father groaned.

"Oh, right. Anne's always trying to pry information, asking if I've said anything about Shania to her friend." She nodded, the spectacles falling forward.

"So they were curious, but never contacted her. Even after Justin was born." A fresh wave of anger roiled through Morgan.

"Pride will be the downfall of that family," his father agreed.

"Remember the first few nights Shania stayed with us? We heard her crying most of the night." Maggie pulled a tissue out of her house-jacket pocket, repositioned her frames and dabbed her eyes. "She tried to keep quiet. Poor dear must have been sobbing into her pillow."

Morgan scrubbed hair away from his face.

"Morgan, if you love Shania and she told you she loved you, why didn't you go to her before now? Track her down the day she left, instead of months later?" Maggie frowned and balled the tissue in her hand.

"I wanted to get rid of Patty first and make sure she wouldn't take me to court or give me grief. I planned to track Shania and go to her this Thursday, when I'm debt free. She's not a risk-taker, so you can imagine my surprise she'd moved. We always talk and now I haven't been able to see…communicate with her."

Maggie sighed. "Well, that's just silly. Can you imagine what that poor girl has been thinking? She probably thinks you don't care about her. Did you tell her you loved her?"

"No. I've asked myself for the past two months why I didn't find her immediately. Many times, I started to drive. I didn't know where to go, but I had to do something. Anything. I've wanted her for so long I kept thinking it was all in my head. Maybe I'd imagined her telling me that she loved me." He rubbed his face with his hands.

"Go see her parents then. If you find out where Shania has moved, you better go prepared. She's going to be angry." His father's bits of wisdom pierced Morgan's heart. Had Shania given up on him? Had he made a mistake by waiting?

Chapter 8

Tuesday came before Shania could catch a breath. One more week of classes and then she'd take finals. In four more days she could close out a CD and have cash. The knots in her stomach eased a little. She'd be able to provide for her son again.

She sat in front of the mirror at the makeshift desk in the tiny foyer applying make-up. Her face appeared whiter and dark circles ringed her eyes. She smoothed the fine skin around her mouth. Laugh lines. The temporary creases would become permanent if she wasn't careful. Her mother always said, "Keep smiling, Shania, and you'll get wrinkles before you're twenty-five." On Saturday, she'd officially be twenty-three and a lotion regimen would be required.

The thump of heels clomping on the hardwood floor brought her fingers, grasping the lip liner, to halt mid-line. She glanced toward the sound. Justin. His booted feet jutted out in wrong directions. Her breath caught in her throat. He was adorable. At his age he didn't have the concept of right and left. "How do the boots feel?"

"Hurt." He sat on the floor and tugged them off.

Shania laughed and turned back to her make-up. "For tonight only, we'll stuff socks inside so you can wear them. If they start to fall off, I'll carry you."

He nodded.

"Go get two socks." She held up two fingers.

He shot off toward the bedroom. Shania stood and straightened the dark blue sweater. She retied the emerald and cyan silk scarf, the geometric shapes adding a whimsical element, then smoothed down the perse-tinted slacks. She stuffed her wallet, lipstick and baby-wipes into her small green bag. Forgetting her cellphone failed to work last Sunday, she reached for it. Even after charging for several hours, she was unable to get the damn thing to function and had given up. She would put the device into the recycling center at the student union next time she went to the West Quad.

Justin ran back into the room, handed her the socks and plopped onto the floor. She rolled the socks, placed one in each boot, then helped Justin pull them on. A smile lit his face as he stood.

"Walk, so we can see if it works." She bit her lip. His other pair of shoes had to be painful to wear. She needed to dress him in boots or slippers. She didn't know where they were going for dinner, but slippers would be frowned upon.

Justin limped for a couple of steps. "My feet move."

The doorbell rang.

"Well, they'll have to do. I'll carry you. All right?" She thought he'd say no. He was getting more independent and difficult to manage, typical for his age although irritating.

"This time."

She mentally sighed and opened the door for Adam. His long black cashmere overcoat hosted was covered with drops of water. A light blue polo shirt peeked from underneath and khakis completed the outfit. His devilish dark eyes glittered as he smiled. The scent of Christmas trees fragranced the air as he got closer to her.

She inhaled, enjoying the pine aroma of his cologne and the presence of a man. "Hi, how are you?"

"Good. And you?" He smiled.

"Is it raining?" She zipped her short-waist black jacket.

"Snowing." His hot gaze made her nervous. She twisted the edge of her scarf.

"Snow?" Justin shouted and awkwardly ran to the window. "Mommy, look."

She strode to the casement and glanced into the overcast night. The side of M2 was visible on the ledge outside the glass. He had a pearlescent mantle and hat. The white moon, hidden behind clouds, allowed a faint light to illustrate large flakes drifting toward Earth. "Beautiful."

"Not as beautiful as you, Shania," Adam whispered in her ear.

Startled, she pivoted, bumping his hard form, then stepped back. He grabbed her arm, preventing a fall. Had she led him on, making him think she was into him? She stifled the anger and mistrust.

What was the harm in having a relationship with Adam?

Morgan.

"Thank you. Ready to go, friend?" She smoothed her hair and straightened the scarf.

He smiled, that charming half-cocked grin, and took her hand in his, leading her to the door. "Yes."

Justin clomped behind them. She stopped, slipped her fingers from Adam's and helped Justin put on his coat and gloves. She hoisted him to rest on her hip.

* * * *

Meat and Boards was a surprising title for a restaurant in a progressively vegetarian society at Briarwood. Splattered across the billboard was a proclamation of live shows. Her stomach quivered in fear. As they walked into the round wooden structure, the scent of roasting meat and some other earthy fragrance she couldn't quite put her finger on wafted through the air. Dinner theatre. Cripes, would it be an interactive event? Shy and awkward in public, she didn't want to be a part of it. She frowned and glanced at the exit and then at Adam. He must have read her thoughts.

"You'll like it, and I know Justin will because they have horses." He tickled Justin's side.

"Horses?" Propped on her hip, he twisted away from Adam's probing fingers, jarring her in the process. Justin looked around the reception area.

A tiny woman, wearing a long green dress with an empire waist, walked toward them. A crown of daisies nestled in her dark brown curls, giving her an authentic medieval aura. "Dr. Raimo, your seats are ready. Follow me please."

He hadn't given his name, indicating he may have arranged the reservations in person or that he came here often. She got an uneasy feeling that she'd been set-up, but for what reason?

They walked through a curling hallway until they came to a wide opening. In front of them was a large arena with stadium seating and a domed roof. Skylights cut into the rough-hued boards allowed visibility to the star-studded universe. A grouping of chairs had been sectioned off with banners and colorful flags.

The Renaissance-garbed woman led them to an enclosed private area. Shania was glad she carried Justin because the floor had wood granules on it, and he'd want to get down and play. The boots would have come off and a pint of sawdust would have been transported to her bedroom later.

The tinkling of music, *Greensleeves*, came from speakers. Shania glanced around to find the source. A bit of black mesh was barely visible hidden among the silken materials lining the walls. She tucked Justin onto a chair pre-set with a booster seat. Adam helped them remove their jackets and took a seat beside Justin. She sat on the other side of her son, at the end of the table.

"This is different." She smiled at Adam and placed her bag beside a steel platter.

"You seemed like an old-fashioned kind of woman, so I thought you'd enjoy the restaurant." His grin should have melted her resistance, unfettering her heart. He was sincere, sweet and very handsome, but she would remain true to Morgan.

Adam was from a good family. He'd often talked of his brothers and sisters affectionately. He had similar interests as she--why couldn't she fall in love with him? Was falling in love charmed? Experiencing puppy love with Beck made her into a woman. Morgan and she created a special bond which superseded friendships. He made her feel whole. No, there wouldn't be a third time. Morgan had her devotion and she remained tethered to him.

"Ladies and gentleman." A man's deep voice resonated through the arena. He held a paper scroll in front of his black belted waist. He was dressed in a knee-length jacket--a beautiful periwinkle blue color--and pants that bloomed out at the thighs. He must have had a microphone attached to his frilly collar as his voice boomed throughout the entire thirty-thousand-square-feet of stadium. Shania glanced around. The lower level seats had filled quickly. The spokesperson continued to explain the amazing feats to be performed by the horses and stunning entertainers.

"The opening will amaze you. Special effects will astound you. Magic exists and will be shared with those who believe. A four-course extravaganza, mouth-watering meal will be delivered to your seat. Of course, in keeping with the time, forks and knives will not be provided." He smacked his lips and pretended to lick his fingers. "With the main course of roasted chicken, wet cloths will be available for you to clean your hands if you so desire."

"Audience participation will be an option during our perfect performances." He rolled the scroll back into its original cylinder shape, the red tassels on the end flapping with the movement. "Thank you, ladies and gents. I'm sure you'll enjoy the show."

He walked to the edge of the ring and flung out his arm, exhibiting the azure lining of his jacket. Trumpet sounds vibrated off the exposed beams and an array of performers entered the stadium. Jugglers were outfitted in gloriously bright cloth--ochre, cerulean blue, brunt umber and cadmium red. Musicians wore Mussini green. Entertainers, garbed in vibrant colors, rode on the backs of white, brown and black horses. The scene made her want to seek out paints and canvas.

Shania glanced at her son. In silence, he took in every scenario presented. He laughed as a jester tossed a ball in his direction. Justin tried to catch the plastic orb, but it bounced to Adam who snatched the globe from the air. He handed the toy to Justin, who clasped it firmly between two hands.

Pale-faced women had feathers coming out of the top of their mile-high hair. The bits of fluff fluttered in the wind as their cart, being pulled by a dapper pair of equines, marched around the showground. Shania looked at Adam. He smiled that confident, told-you-so smile. She leaned around Justin and touched Adam's wrist.

"Thank you. You've provided me with a wonderful surprise." Her fingers pressed into the cloth at his wrist.

His eyes clouded with lust. She jerked her hand back. He frowned and reached into his coat.

"I'd thought to give you this during dessert, but why wait?" He extracted a rectangle-shaped package, with a large white ribbon sporting a bow on top. "Happy birthday, Shania."

She closed her eyes, wishing the tears would not roll over. It had been such a long time since she'd received a present that the idea that someone considered her enough to celebrate the day and in such a lovely way overwhelmed her. The dinner, the thoughtfulness--Adam was, without a doubt, a very good person.

"Shania?" Adam asked.

"Mommy?" Justin touched her arm as it rested on the table.

"Sorry, I'm so touched by your thoughtfulness. Thank you, Adam." She took the red foil package. "How did you know?"

He blushed and looked away. "Ah, paperwork."

She ignored the implications that he'd nosed through her medical records and opened the gift. A state of the art cellphone was inside the package. She held it up for inspection. Could she ever learn how to use the darn thing?

"I have the box and instructions in the trunk of my car. If you take the phone to an agent, he'll connect you with your old number. You'll have to enter your entire contact list in again, and you'll have text ability. Also--" He wiggled his fingers in a give-it-over motion.

She handed him the cell.

"This device has internet capabilities, including GPS." He pressed a few buttons and a browser came onto the screen.

She swallowed. How could she afford the monthly utility for the phone? If he'd arranged service in advance, she wouldn't dream of allowing him to pay. He shut the device down and handed it to her. She could smell his pine-scented cologne on the cellular.

"Thank you," she croaked and placed the mobile in her purse.

The first course of bread and cheese was placed in front of them, giving her time to think about how to refuse the gift or, barring that, exchanging the phone for a less expensive version. She'd deal with the conundrum later. Now, she wanted to bask in the glow of a wonderful evening with her friend and her son.

She stole a glance at Adam during the chicken course. He was nice and cared about Justin. Why couldn't she accept him as a possible partner? As a guy who had dating and a future in mind? He said he planned to settle down and get married. Although her lungs constricted at the thought, her mind wanted to embrace him and his obvious goals.

Adam was an excellent doctor, kind and considerate--all good qualities in a prospective partner. He could get any woman he desired. Why was he interested in her?

Dessert arrived. Clanking of metal against metal came from her right. She pushed the apple turnover away as she saw the snout of a stallion out of the corner of her eye. This wouldn't be good. A knight, wearing full polished silver armor, rode his equine close to their raised table. Laughter and whispers sprinkled around her. Crap, audience participation. She wasn't getting on that animal in front of spectators. The beautiful steed blew out a puff of air as if in retribution for her thoughts. He smelled of earthy hay. Oat-scented air filtered into her nose as he blew out another breath. She loved horses. Memories of helping Morgan's father groom his stock came flooding back as this beast lifted his head in a nod.

"My Lady." The knight's gruff baritone voice pierced the air. He lifted the shield on the mask, exposing his lower face.

Shania resisted the urge to glance behind her. Maybe he intended the address to someone else. Nope. He dismounted and awkwardly maneuvered near her chair. Thank goodness a solid six foot wall was between them. Adam urged her to acknowledge the knight.

A poignant silence fell over the crowd, making her more uncomfortable.

"I'm about to go into contest with the evil Dark Knight. Might I have a bit of goodwill? Perhaps a token of your favor to wear upon my helm?" His deep voice rang through the arena. He pointed a gloved hand toward her.

The crowd roared, shouting, "Give him a token."

"Shania, give him your scarf," Adam encouraged.

Her face heated. She smiled and unknotted the emerald scarf from her neck. Quickly rising, she walked around her chair, down a set of stairs, and handed the cloth to the knight.

"My Lady, garbed as such, I'll need your assistance. Please." He winked at her. Scratches screeched through the speakers as he twisted to get closer.

She leaned on the wooden rail. He shifted his lance to his other hand and held out his arm. She tied her scarf around his bicep below the tin cap of the sleeve, as applause came from the onlookers. The knight bowed. He mounted his horse with such ease, obviously he performed this act every night.

He saluted the audience. "Thank you, my Lady."

The white knight slammed down the cheek plate, the bevor standing out strong and sharp, and rode to the opposite side of the arena. Shania took a sip of mead--a diet cream soda--and kept her eyes focused on the table. Beck was the last male to request an item of clothing from her. As the play continued, metal clanked against metal and Shania catapulted back to the day she was with Beck, the day he left her forever.

* * * *

Beck, Morgan and Shania stood at the entry of the airport concourse. Beck would exit through the gates and be gone for a whole year. Perhaps during that time he'd get a military leave and they could plan their marriage, unless his parents convinced him otherwise. The engagement announcement during dinner at their house hadn't gone as well as she had hoped. As Shania had expected, shards of hate radiated from his mother's sharp blue eyes.

"I know the announcement didn't go as well as I'd hoped. They'll like you--eventually. Keep going to my house and talk to them." Beck dropped his carry-on and hugged her.

Morgan stepped to the side and glanced out the windows toward the tarmac.

"They hate me, Beck. I'm not going to barge in uninvited." She pressed her hand against his firm chest, missing him already. Thank goodness classes started next week. She'd become immersed in studying and time would quickly pass.

"No, they don't. They're just surprised." He winked at Morgan.

What the heck? Had Beck confided in Morgan that his parents didn't like her? She bit her lip to keep from speaking out.

"Morgan, I expect you to take care of my brown-eyed girl. Promise?" Beck clapped Morgan on the back.

Morgan drew him into a hug and nodded. "Sure, I promise to take care of Shania until you're able to once again."

"Good, I know you will." Beck tightened his lips. Had something passed between them before the promise and he was reaffirming?

Beck released his friend. "Good luck with your business ventures. I'm sure you'll be successful. You've got a bright mind behind that ugly mug."

"Peace be with you, my friend," Morgan said. His tone had a rasp, like metal wheels rubbing dryly against each other.

"Same here," Beck replied, his voice solemn and low-pitched. He grabbed Shania. "Now, my love, I hope you'll favor me with a token. Something with your scent on it."

Tongue sliding across his lips, he slyly winked, making the sweet thought turn naughty and nasty, reminding her of his desire for her to talk dirty during sex.

She removed her neck scarf. She'd selected the cloth because it matched Beck's indigo eyes perfectly. Hands shaking, she tied the token around his neck. "Here's good luck to my future husband. Return safely to me."

Beck never returned to her.

* * * *

"My Lady," a baritone voice proclaimed.

Shania returned to the present. Chanting came from the stands behind her and pounded through her mind. She glanced around the dusty arena and at the people shouting. What did they want her to do?

She shook her head as the deep voice repeated, "My Lady?"

She glanced at the knight holding onto the reins of a sweating horse. Bejeweled jesters danced in the background. Suddenly, the scent of grilled meat made her gag.

She looked to the right and to the left searching for an escape. Cheering crowds blurred her vision. The clash and hurtle of the reenacted joust had passed and now the white knight stood in front of her. His horse pawed the ground beside him. The cheek plate of his closed-helmet lifted, his brown eyes searching hers.

"I have won the tournament and present to you a token of my esteem." He held a large silver ring the size of her palm. The plastic diamond shimmered under the bright lights.

Hoots and whistles were shouted. She glanced at Adam. He smiled and nodded toward the guy's extended hand. She went down the stairs and stood at the railing, curtseyed as best as possible inside a booth with pants on, and took the ring. "Thank you, sir. I accept your gift."

The handsome, silver-clad guardian climbed onto the saddle and waved to the audience. Her green scarf, still attached to his arm, fluttered in the breeze. The other performers made a final round, receiving a standing ovation and ending the show. Shania stuffed the oversized ring into her bag. Cameras flashed from every direction. She needed to leave. The urgency was so extreme her legs became jelly and her arms shook.

She helped Justin put on his coat and zipped it. As she snuggled into her light-weight jacket, Adam picked up her son and then took her sweaty palm into his. They missed the mad rush to the exits due to their box seats. Her pulse continued its erratic rate. Why did snippets of her past keep invading her thoughts?

The ride to her place was quiet. What could she say? Adam's thoughtfulness and generosity overwhelmed her. Instead of overanalyzing, she should appreciate his behaviors as they were intended...acts of kindness. The night did indeed have a magical quality, as the orator claimed. She closed her eyes. The evening would have been perfect had Morgan been there.

Adam carried Justin to her apartment, his tiny red boots flopping up and down. Shania slipped the ball and large ring from her purse, found the keys and replaced the items. She opened the door and turned to Adam.

"Let me carry him inside," Adam whispered. She led the way to the bedroom. He laid Justin on top of his youth bed and glanced around. Embarrassed about their simple, humble living conditions, Shania made quick work of removing Justin's boots and outer garments, and covered him with his coveted Bob the Builder blanket.

Together Adam and Shania walked out of the bedroom. Was this the process of a married couple tucking their child in at night? She didn't have a frame of reference as she couldn't recall her parents wishing her good night. For the past year, her dreams were always of Morgan, tucking Justin in bed and then her later.

"Thank you, Adam, for such a lovely night and especially for the birthday gift," she whispered.

"It was my pleasure, Shania." He placed his hand on the side of her face. "That's what friends do for each other, in addition to becoming close, like family."

Adam's mouth lightly brushed hers. His eyes closed when he kissed her. Soft lips pressed against hers with a feathery touch, making him all the more charming and the smooch all the more harmless.

Not finding opposition he leaned closer. His tongue touched her lips. Friends didn't French. She broke the lip lock.

"Good night," she said and strolled to the door. Should she give the phone back and make it very clear she did not desire a romantic relationship or continue as-is, wading through his not-so-obvious manipulations? Or should she remove the restraints from her emotions and accept another man in her life, a guy she could possibly come to like?

Chapter 9

The Village, a block from campus, held modern commerce as well as a traditional barbershop and antique store. Cell-Station stood out in its angular contemporary glory among rustic buildings and hundred-year-old trees. Shania walked out of the thriving wireless business and situated into a quiet shaded spot along the sidewalk, braced against the limestone wall. She pushed a button. The entry was deleted instead of saved. Damn, would she ever figure out how to use the phone?

Her bag bumped into the side of the stone as she settled more comfortably against the rock face. She entered three numbers into the memory bank: Morgan, daycare and Megan. Adam had already entered his contact information. He'd also paid the first year of service in advance. The present was a nice gesture, as long as it was a token of friendship. Logically, she needed a phone. She always wanted to be in contact with Justin. Besides, she did enjoy having a male friend and Adam fit the role perfectly.

Shania feared being hurt by another man. Like a thief, Beck had stolen all of her ability to trust in love. Her essence had been stifled because of his duplicity, but not purloined. Her love for Morgan catapulted her into a new dimension. No rebounding would be in her future. Her world revolved around Justin and her artwork, and she'd be contented with those.

* * * *

The doorbell had to have been created by Whitechapel Bell Foundry, the makers of Big Ben. The vibrations literally shook the Miller's steel entrance. Morgan had been an Indiana Scholar which had awarded him a trip to London, so he was familiar with that particular chime. He straightened the collar of his black polo and brushed the lint from his suede jacket. His mantra, "Shania loves you", continued to replay in his mind. He hoped he hadn't waited too long.

An older woman wearing a white starched hat and black dress answered the door.

"I need to see Mr. or Mrs. Miller please."

"Please come in." She lowered her gaze to the tile floor.

"Who is it, Mary?" Mrs. Miller's voice didn't resemble her daughter's, although her face and form could be confused for an older version of Shania. Shania would age beautifully. If Morgan could convince Shania to marry him, he vowed to walk through the stages of life with her at his side.

Morgan stepped across the threshold and held out his hand. "I'm Morgan Hardwick."

The bracelets at her wrist jangled, creating a ting-ting melody as Mrs. Miller held out her palm and shook his hand.

The door shut quietly behind him.

"Thank you, Mary."

Mary, quietly dismissed, hurried away.

"I know who you are, Mr. Hardwick. Your father took care of my daughter's horse when it had a fungus on its foot. Is Dr. Hardwick still a practicing veterinarian?"

"Retirement is pending. Thank you for asking." His mouth was suddenly dry. A quick swipe of tongue over his lips didn't help.

"Come into the parlor. May I take your coat?" She hadn't smiled. If he were to attach one word to Shania's mother it would be stoic.

"No, thank you. I'll just take a moment of your time." He took a deep breath, inhaling an apple scent. Her perfume or the aroma coming from the potpourri in the glass dish on the half-round oak table wafted, scenting the foyer.

"Tell me why you stopped by our home this bright November day." She pointed to the first doorway on the left of the entrance hall. Pearl carpet. He walked inside the room. Except for the silver accent pieces, the entire space looked like a snow fort as it was decorated in all-white furniture. A flood of sympathy enveloped him, thinking of a tiny Shania properly sitting on the sofa instead of lounging among friends talking crap about boys.

He sat on the edge of the couch. Mrs. Miller sashayed to a side bar and lifted the shiny cap from an ice bucket. "Drink, Mr. Hardwick?"

He grit his teeth. It was ten in the morning. Was she a lush? "No, thank you. I have a morning appointment, so I'll get right to my reason for being here."

She dropped the lid in place. Without preparing a beverage, she glided to the settee, and sat down. "Please do."

He had to make his request in clear logical terms, without emotion. "Shania has left Cyan and I need to find her. Do you know where she's gone?" Sap!

Her lips tightened and her eyes narrowed. "No. I haven't talked to Shania since she got pregnant, lied to us and the Longviews. That was four years ago, I believe."

"She never lied to you." Morgan's stomach turned and twisted. The pounding in his chest escalated as if he'd climbed several flights of stairs. He would not allow the Millers to believe the fabrications provided by the Longviews. They'd forgotten how to tell the truth.

"I beg to differ, but I'm not going to go into it with you. Did you see today's paper?" She smiled as if she'd taken a bite from a bitter apple.

"Not yet." He hated how his voice sounded scratchy. Despite her intimidating manner, he wanted to make a good impression. He planned to marry her daughter.

Mrs. Miller went into the foyer. Her heels clacked on the wood floors. Then the sound of a drawer opening and shutting. It clicked in place and her heels tapped as she returned. She handed him a rectangular announcement cut from newsprint.

"Beck Longview and Taffy Canterbury are announcing their upcoming wedding on December twentieth." She pointed to a paragraph in the middle. "They were officially engaged in July 2004, but the groom left to serve his country."

Mrs. Miller slithered to the sofa, sat and crossed her legs. Morgan finished reading the article detailing the time, date and place for Beck's wedding. He slowly removed his wallet. The photo he sought was the first thing visible whenever he opened his billfold.

He slid the picture of Justin beside Beck's, placing it on top of Taffy's sharp-boned face and red-blond hair, and carried the items to Mrs. Miller. "Shania never lied. Beck did love her in his own way. She waited three years for him, staying loyal to him the entire time." He handed her the two images. "As you can see Beck fathered your grandson, Justin, as they look so much alike…but Mrs. Miller…"

She clutched the newsprint and photo in her hand and lifted her head. Her hard shell, maybe due to the truth, had broken, aging her. Water hovered at the corners of her eyes.

"I am his father. If you should hear anything, I'd like to be advised. You know how to reach me." He held out his hand to collect the photograph.

"May I keep the photo of my grandson?" Her voice cracked.

Morgan hesitated. He didn't want to let go of the picture. He might need it to locate Justin and Shania. Mrs. Miller's face paled and tears tracked down her red cheeks, smearing her make-up.

"Yes," he whispered, slid his wallet into his pocket, pivoted, and walked to the door.

"Mr. Hardwick." Her tear-choked voice ripped through the room.

He stopped and glanced at her.

"We are Shania's base address at Briarwood University. A few days ago we got an overdue notice for tuition. You might be able to locate her on campus." She crumbled the newspaper announcement and held the photo of Justin to her chest.

Morgan would tie up loose ends and go to Briarwood today.

* * * *

Chaotic Thursday arrived before she could turn around. Tired from too little sleep, she glanced at the clock in the square as she rushed to get Justin home from daycare. Because of his tight footwear, Justin didn't complain about being carried or unable to explore on their way home as was the norm. Guilt pierced her gut. On Saturday she'd have a mature CD and straightaway she'd buy him a pair of shoes.

Shania unlocked the door to their apartment, crossed over the threshold leaving the entrance open as she removed Justin's too small athletic shoes, and lowered him to the floor.

"Shania." Her dream lover's voice caressed her skin.

Breath caught in her throat, she pivoted. "Morgan," she whispered as air finally flowed from her lungs.

* * * *

Shania dropped her bags, and to Morgan's surprise hurled herself into his arms. She tucked her face into the nook of his neck and inhaled. He closed his eyes and held onto her, not wanting to ever let go.

"I've missed…you." His voice faltered.

"Daddy," Justin shouted and ran forward, arms outstretched.

Morgan lowered Shania, keeping an arm around her waist. Eyes watering, he grabbed Justin, snuggling him close to his chest. He hadn't fully comprehended how much the two of them meant to him. Never again would he take their love, their presence for granted.

A single tear leaked down Shania's face. She turned away. "Let's go inside."

He released her waist. She led the way into the living room. Justin clung to Morgan as he shut the door, cocooning them.

"Sit, please. Would you like a drink?" She pointed to a sofa, then used her forearm to swipe at her face.

Unsure what to do or say, he shifted Justin to the other hip. She wouldn't appreciate him mentioning the tears.

"No, thank you," Morgan responded. With Justin glued to his side, Morgan walked around the apartment, looking at how she'd decorated. An easel had been set in the corner. The work in progress was covered with a bed sheet. Everything was in its place, neat and tidy. Some of her habits hadn't changed in the last two months.

"I go to school now," Justin said.

"You do?" Morgan touched the side of the face he so loved.

"I have a friend named Sam." Justin clung to Morgan's jacket.

Morgan smoothed his hair, reassuring him he'd heard him.

"Why are you here?" Shania asked. Her eyes glassy, she looked around, anywhere but at him. Had he caused those snuffles? Were they tears of joy or remorse?

"I got a call on Friday, although you didn't leave a message. I've dialed your number every day. No answer." He glanced into the bedroom to see two beds, one small, almost a cot. His knotted stomach muscles twisted with anxiousness, wanting to share her pallet, fearing she didn't call because there was someone new. If there was another man in her life, this time Morgan would fight for her.

He hadn't wanted to contact her until his debts were eliminated and he could begin a permanent relationship. Part of his reluctance to seek her was his anger. She'd waited until minutes before he was to commit to another before approaching him. Why couldn't she have shared her feelings at any time during the past three years?

He'd subdued the irritation of her inappropriate timing and the remorse because he'd almost achieved his goal.

All he had to do was confirm their shared love. Hopefully it wasn't too late for them. His body chilled with fear—he'd forgiven her, but had he waited too long?

"Yes, I did call. My phone broke." She sat down on the stool in front of a rocker--the chair they had used to soothe Justin asleep for the first couple of years of his life. She stared, evaluating him like a psychology experiment, making him question his delayed actions again.

Morgan walked to the sofa and sat down, propping Justin on his lap. "Did you get it fixed?"

"No, Adam gave me a new one." She hadn't moved her gaze from his face. Her scrutiny unnerved him and excited him at the same time. Had he glimpsed a smidgen of longing, of love, in her cat eyes?

Mouth dry, he licked his lips. "Who's Adam?"

"A friend." She clasped her hands, her knuckles showed white. "How's Patty?"

"She's the same." He tugged off Justin's coat. The dark blue sweatshirt had lifted. Morgan pulled Justin's sweatshirt down, tickling the soft tummy skin as he did. Justin giggled but didn't push Morgan's hand away as he would have done in the past.

"How was the honeymoon? Did you like Aruba?" She frowned, as if she regretted the question. In the next instant she smiled. Her eyes held sadness and possibly anger, but at herself or him he didn't know.

"There wasn't a honeymoon, Shania. We didn't get married." He lowered Justin to the floor. Hot and irritated, Morgan stood and removed his wool overcoat, keeping his gaze on her, needing to see her reaction to the announcement. "I planned to explain everything after I settled accounts with Patty, but you left and--"

The doorbell rang. Shania glanced at the black round wall clock and then to the door. Had he lost the opportunity to explain?

"Megan, the babysitter," she said in explanation and stood.

Justin sat on the floor running a truck over a bump on the stained brown carpet.

Cramps ripped through Morgan's gut. He had waited too long to contact her. He'd lost her. "You have a date?"

"No, I have night class. Megan from down the hall comes every Thursday to stay with Justin." The doorbell sounded again, longer and shrill.

"Could I stay with him tonight? He's changed so much." He propped his hands on his hips. His heart rate climbed to a fearful speed, as if he ascended the side of a mountain.

"It's been more than two months. Children change. People change." Her tone had a bite of acid. Quick change, although he was glad she outwardly showed irritation. Hate and love were a fine thread away from each other. Anger wasn't part of her personality or her normal reactions, so this emotion must have been stewing for a few weeks. Deep down, he knew she still cared for him. He hadn't lost.

"Shania, please allow me to explain." He stood. Morgan's change in tone from happy to anxious must have alerted Justin because he crawled on all fours and clasped Morgan's leg.

She glanced at Justin. The child held his arms tight to Morgan's thigh and pressed his cheek against the cold jeans. She shifted her gaze to meet his. Justin wanted to stay with him. Would she let him? His breath caught in his throat as he waited for her decision. He wished they could always remain together, a family of three.

"Okay." She ran to the door. A jerk of the brass knob flung her backward as the entrance flew open.

"I was worried. You always answer on the first ring. What's going on?" A black-haired teen, decked in a bright pink loose top and pants, stood with legs braced and hands resting on her non-existent hips. Her dark-eyed glance met his. Various facial piercings shimmered in the light. "Hi, I'm Megan."

"I'm Morgan Hardwick." He bent, released Justin's arms from their tight grip and picked him up.

"My daddy," Justin added.

Megan stared at the trio, analyzing Morgan as if he were a puzzle. "For real?"

Justin nodded. Shania sucked in her breath.

"Gosh, Shania, I didn't know Justin knew the word. He's never said that before." Megan stepped forward, hand outstretched.

Morgan met her halfway and shook her small hand. "Thanks for taking care of my son."

"Excuse me." Shania sounded as if she were choking. She took a deep breath, then ran into the bathroom.

"Megan, if you don't mind, I'm going to stay with Justin tonight." Morgan tried to put Justin on the sofa, but he clung like a monkey to a banana tree. He shifted the boy to his other hip and reached into his back pocket. "Let me give you something, so you can enjoy your night off."

"That's buck." She smiled, accepted the twenty, and shouted, "Shania, you all right in there?"

"Yes. Sorry, Megan. I'll talk to you tomorrow. Thank you." Her suddenly nasal voice came from the other side of the door.

Morgan's heart wrenched. He'd done that, made her cry.

"See ya, buddy," Megan said to Justin. She winked, making the pink ball on her eyebrow move. She turned with a dramatic flair and bounced out of the apartment.

"Bye, Megan," Justin shouted, kicking his stocking feet against Morgan's thigh.

Morgan placed him on the carpet. "I'll be right back. Get your trucks out and we'll play."

Justin nodded and scampered, gathering his toys.

Morgan went to the bathroom and knocked lightly. The sniffles indicated Shania was upset. He was the reason, and he needed to sort the various threads to help unravel the mess. "May I come in?"

Shania opened the door and glanced at Morgan, then Justin. He'd flipped on the television. A cartoon played on the screen. She took a step back and Morgan entered, shutting the wood until the latch clicked.

He grabbed her and tucked his face into the nook of her neck and shoulder. She allowed him to stroke her back. He breathed in her essence. "What's wrong?"

"Justin said Daddy," she mumbled into his shirt collar. Her muscles relaxed.

"You don't want him to call me...that?" He couldn't say the word. When the child of his heart shouted "Daddy" he'd nearly collapsed. In his dreams he'd envisioned them as a family, with Shania referring to him as husband and Justin labeling him Daddy. Her snow-white face led him to believe his wish might not come true. Had Shania found another father for Justin? His gut tightened in pain. In the past two months had she found someone to entitle partner or lover?

"No, I'm surprised and happy. You have been a father to him. It's normal for Justin to love the people he sees the most and who take care of him. Are you okay with him calling you Daddy?" She backed away, but maintained eye contact with him. A tear glimmered on her right cheekbone.

"Yes." He caressed the side of her face, wiping away the tear and smoothing her short hair behind her ears. A touch of her lips to his. He'd loved her for the past four years and never once had their mouths connected. Fear he wouldn't stop with a simple brush had always prevented him from approaching her and joining their souls. He wanted to kiss her. She was unattached and they were free to be together. He loved her. Morgan leaned—

Light taps sounded on the door. "I need to potty."

She turned her cheek, breaking the spell. "And I need to go to class. Monsieur Barrett shuts the door and doesn't let students, arriving late, inside."

Morgan swiped his hand through his hair. Their first kiss shouldn't happen in a bathroom anyway. He opened the door, letting Justin enter.

She bent down and kissed Justin's forehead. "I need to rush. Be good. I'll be back after class, around ten."

She slid beside Morgan and exited the tight space. Morgan left the door ajar, rushed forward, and grabbed her hand. "Skip class, spend the night with us."

"I can't. Next week is the final." She released his hand, lifted two bags, and headed to the door. "Morgan, there's juice and whatever he wants to eat in the fridge. Here, let me get you a key in case you want to go out later. The apartment closes-in fast, so a breath of air helps. Do you have a car seat?"

He nodded.

"The area's safe, but on Thursday night the parties commence." She dug into her purse, her fingers deep in the contents, and came up with a brass house key.

He took the token, holding his fingers against hers for a longer period than necessary. "We need to talk."

"Tonight." She glanced at the clock, grabbed her backpack and rushed out the door.

A small hand slid across his palm. He glanced down at Justin. "Looks like it's just you and me, kid."

"Juice?" Justin asked.

"Sure." Hands clasped, they walked to the fridge. Morgan shoved the key into his pocket and pulled the door open. The light bulb glared at them in the nearly empty refrigerator. Two small cups were on the left side of the shelf. On the right side were a half gallon of low-fat milk, a liter of apple juice and two containers of yogurt.

A loaf of bread, jam and organic peanut butter occupied the second shelf.

He let the door close and had a strong urge to go through the cupboards to see if she had any food. Sadness at seeing a nearly empty fridge and pantry made his gut clutch. He'd let them down. Thankfully Mrs. Miller gave him the clue about Briarwood, so he'd called and tracked Shania's address through student services.

Morgan mentally kicked himself for not being available when they needed him. "Would you like to go out to dinner?"

"See horses?" Justin asked.

"I don't know. Where are your shoes?" Morgan led him to the sofa. "Oh, there they are."

Morgan grabbed the small pair of shoes and carried them to Justin. "Here you go."

"No, they hurt." Justin pushed his hands against them.

"Son, if you want to go into a restaurant you'll have to wear something on your feet. No shirt, no shoes, no service." He tickled the bottom of Justin's soles. Giggles echoed through the room. A child's laughter was something he'd truly missed. He'd fight for Shania and Justin. They would legally become a family.

Morgan slid the shoes onto Justin's feet and understood. The boy had grown and the footwear was too small.

"Do you have other shoes?"

"Boots." Justin pointed to his bedroom.

Morgan went into the small room and noticed a pair of red boots up against the end of the cot. They looked twice the size of the athletic shoes. He walked out to Justin, who remained on the sofa swinging his feet.

"Why don't we get you new shoes and then go to dinner?"

Justin nodded. Morgan slipped the shoes onto Justin's feet, leaving the center open so he'd have a slight flex space. After helping Justin put on his coat and hat, Morgan zipped his own, tugged the apartment key out of his pants pocket and locked the door. He gathered Justin into his arms and carried him down the stairs.

His pickup truck held a metered space outside the building. Ten minutes left on the time. He'd park down the block in an overnight parking structure when they returned. He settled Justin on the child's carrier beside him and placed the seatbelt around the little hips. Morgan hoped--planned--for Shania and Justin to return with him, so the booster seat was in place.

"Don't move around because I need to concentrate on driving. Okay?"

Justin nodded, glanced at the dials of the radio, and crossed his arms.

Morgan disliked a shopping center with a passion. However, by going to a mall he could achieve both goals of getting footwear and food. He parked his truck and helped Justin out of the vehicle. He carried him into the nearest shoe store. Justin selected a pair with lights on the edges of the soles that glowed when he ran throughout the shop. He stomped his feet, keeping his gaze glued to the mirrors along the way.

The gray-haired salesperson squinted behind his black plastic eyeglasses. His white shirt had a nametag embossed with Dave. He handed Morgan an empty box inside a plastic bag. "Here's your change. Do you want me to toss the old ones?"

"Yes, thanks, Dave." Morgan took the sack.

"He'll be a hit on the playground. We just got the shoes today. They're trainers for tots, to teach them to run properly. You know, heel to toe. Heel lights up green for go. Toe has a yellow light for caution." He dropped the tiny, worn-out pair in a trash bin at the side of the counter.

"Sounds like a nice idea." Morgan glanced around for Justin. "Come on, Justin. We'll get some chow."

Justin screamed in glee as they passed by a restaurant with a large mouse on the billboard. The inside of the eatery resembled a carnival with toys, games and loud music. Pizza was delivered on a large round pie pan, with cheese resembling glue and tasting like rubber. The clang-clang of the pinball machines added to Morgan's distaste for the environment. Kids ran around, playing video games, jumping in a cage filled with balls. By the time they walked out of the germ-infested mousetrap, Morgan was exhausted. He choked back the tomato sauce caught in his craw.

They exited the mall and climbed into his truck. Morgan strapped Justin to his car seat. "Let's go to the market and get some apples and bananas. Are you up for one more stop?"

"Sure. See horses?" He bounced his heels against the edge of the car seat and clapped his hands together. The sugar high from Mouse-Critter cotton candy was still running through the little guy's system.

"Maybe." At the market Morgan intended to get fruit and vegetables, but Justin ran ahead, tossing items into the cart. Aware that Shania preferred organic or natural foods, he put most of the products Justin chose back on the shelf.

Morgan checked out, stowed the goods in the back and drove to Shania's apartment. He parked in the garage, lifted the bags into one hand and clasped Justin's fingers with the other. Justin's steps were slow and lethargic. The sugar buzz had worn off.

Unlocking the door proved to be a challenge as he balanced several sacks. He lowered the bags inside the door, shucked his coat and picked up Justin's from where he'd shed it. The groceries were shoved into the fridge.

Justin lay on the floor, his head resting on an outstretched arm, and moved a truck over the carpet. Morgan went into the bathroom and started the water to fill the tub.

"Come on, kid, you'll take a bath and then to bed. I'm sure it's later than your usual time." He rolled up his shirt sleeves.

Justin dropped the truck in the middle of the floor and entered the bathroom.

He glanced into the clear pool. "Bubbles?"

Morgan turned off the faucet. From past experience, he knew Justin would play in bubbles for a long time. "How about tomorrow? I'm very tired. Tonight we'll do a quick clean and off to bed."

"Okay." He sat on the floor and tugged off his shoes. A green light sparkled as a sole hit the linoleum.

Morgan helped him remove his clothes, then lifted him over the edge of the tub. He squeezed liquid from a bottle of bath wash onto a sponge shaped like a square with facial features, trousers and a red tie.

"Adam bought your mom a new phone?"

Justin nodded, keeping his attention on swirling the water.

"Do you like Adam?" Morgan didn't like himself for asking, but he had to know. He smashed the gum-scented soap onto the necktie of the sponge's imprinted outfit. With gentleness he reserved for his son, he removed the evening's germs from his unknowing revealer of information.

"Yes." Justin yawned. His hand created an eddy through the water.

Morgan rinsed him. He should come out and ask, "Does he come often? Has he stayed overnight?"

"Okay, buddy, out you go. We'll get you tucked in." Morgan grabbed a towel from the basket next to the tub. He wanted to know if the man kissed Shania, yet he didn't.

He wrapped a towel around Justin, then carried him into the bedroom. Dressed and under the covers, Justin's eyelids shuttered closed as fast as the bathwater drained.

Morgan went into the bathroom, stripped and jumped into the tub. He pulled the gold curtain. He quickly removed the stench of pizza using Shania's vanilla-scented liquid soap. How should he approach her? Out of the shower, he used a towel from the bar to tap dry. Morgan's jeans stuck to his wet skin. Snatching his shirt, socks and loafers off the floor, he gathered Justin's soiled clothing and shoes. Burdened with garments, he strode into the living room.

Had another man entered their lives while Morgan followed his own code of honor? He placed his long sleeve button-down on the sofa arm and dropped his work boots. Next he dumped Justin's clothes in the hamper and placed the new shoes beside the bed. Morgan padded behind the cleverly painted curtain to glance out the window. The quad was alive with activity--guys hanging in a crowd, women wrapping their arms around the men's waists, trying to draw attention. One female danced in circles on the dew-capped lawn.

The scene took him back to his youth, as a student on campus. A mere five years later he felt old and tired of being alone. Tired of loving a woman who continued to be out of reach. He glanced at her bed. Had another man occupied the space beside the woman he loved? No, he couldn't see her taking a lover to bed in the same room as Justin. Her character wouldn't allow her to be with someone without a commitment in place. Morgan laid on the edge of her bed, breathing in her woman scent, a combination of vanilla and Shania. He was so very tired.

Chapter 10

Shania grabbed the edge of the classroom door right before it closed. Students hovered around seats chatting, comparing notes. Others removed their sketches from the rectangular cubicles and placed them on easels. The room had a charcoal graphite aroma instead of the pleasant oil paint scents she'd become fond of and accustomed to. She'd wanted to be an artist from the time she experienced finger-painting in primary school. The desire to craft had never faltered. No constricting of strings with painting. Love of art was a constant in her ever-changing life.

Monsieur Barrett bowed his head in acknowledgement. "Miss Miller."

His dour facial expression made her reconsider going home to be with Justin and Morgan. A spark of anger resided in Monsieur's eyes, making her stomach quiver in unknowing fear.

"I'm sorry for being late," she said and slid past him.

"I need to see you after class," he replied. His voice resonated throughout the room. "Class, open your Fillwalk text to chapter twelve. William Morris Hunt's life revolved around melancholy and a sense of isolation."

Shania could relate to Hunt's emotional trauma, both of them experienced sadness and self-imposed separation from people, individuals she regarded as family.

"Hunt had a vision as a painter, as all of us do. He joined other artists specializing in the country's finest landscape painting."As professor Barrett's monotone voice continued discussing an American drawing group, Shania mentally related to the sense of loneliness.

Solitude and expression. Like Hunt, Shania had secluded herself from the world to some extent, and she'd been downright miserable until two hours ago. Morgan had returned to them. What would her future hold? Would he become a part of their lives--permanently?

"Thomas Cole's *Study of a Blasted Tree* inspires isolation similar to Hunt. The broken and desolate peaks of granite and deep seclusion of the tangled woods describe his thoughts of pathless solitude." The professor stood beside her seat.

Shania understood pathless solitude in regards to her relationships. She wandered aimlessly trying to determine what choices would create harmony in her life. Materialistically, goals had been set. Responsibilities were always present, but what about love? She'd loved two men. Beck had declared his love, yet never exhibited faith and loyalty. Beck's parents probably had someone they wanted him to marry. Obviously Beck had lied to the other woman as well, since he was engaged to both at them for a period of time. Funny she never ran into the blonde when she visited Beck. Regardless, he'd gotten what he wanted. She couldn't be angry with Beck because their engagement had been a win-win situation. He'd been relieved of whatever he'd wanted to flee for that short amount of time, and she'd become a mother.

She existed because of Justin. Regardless of what he did in the future, she'd never abandon her son. Giving her love to her child and to Morgan proved to be like a landscape painting, highs and lows using different textures at every level.

"The canvas confines a moment of silence and mystery as the obstacle is breached." Monsieur Barrett tapped the top of the desk, bringing her out of her musings. "Miss Miller, name another artist who creates a harmony between nature, humans and landscapes."

Crap. She shouldn't have been focusing on her own problems rather than listening to the professor's recapping of the old material.

"Homer?"

"Good guess, Miss Miller. Winslow Homer, a semi-solitude artist, was lured by nature." Monsieur strolled back to the front of the classroom.

Her focus remained on the professor, while her mind continued its journey down Morgan Lane. She had hope in her life that loneliness would be in her past, because an unmarried Morgan was back in their lives. What had he told the wedding guests? Was Shania's reputation more exposed and dirty than it had been? No, if Morgan made the announcement, he wouldn't have said anything negative. Patty? Yes, she would have freely trash-talked Shania.

Did Morgan love her? Would he tell her tonight?

If he did, he'd surely have contacted her before now. Morgan's high morals and strong sense of responsibility would obligate him. More than likely, he couldn't reach her due to her broken phone. His upstanding character would lead him to Briarwood to determine if she and Justin were okay. She hadn't thought about it before this second, but just because he didn't marry Patty didn't mean he'd ended the engagement. Ah, that thought was certainly a new texture to the "love" mural.

Her pulse shot to a fast speed, keeping time with the professor's click of the power point. Could Morgan still be engaged? Instead of sketching in Morgan, Justin and her, the fantastic lovescape could be comprised of only Justin and her--semi-solitude.

"Ladies and gentlemen, next week the final will be brutal. Bring your A-game." Monsieur Barrett shut off his laptop. The projection showed a blue screen. "Unless you have questions, you're excused."

Shania sluggishly loaded her bag with her books, pen and highlighter. Her classmates hurried out of the room. She placed the strap on her shoulder and picked up her portfolio. Barrett handed out graded work and Shania stuffed the papers inside the case. The A on her work didn't matter. Monsieur's decision about Justin's art was more important.

He stood close enough his breath moved hair onto her face. "Shania, come into my office."

She glanced at the wall clock, nine fifty. Fist tight around the bag handles, she followed him. He indicated for her to sit. Sliding onto the hardwood chair, she dropped the carriers to the floor, and folded her hands in her lap.

"Did you instruct Justin on still life?" Monsieur Barrett's eyes glittered with delight. His mouth, which she'd once believed to be a permanent frown, changed into a semi-smile.

"Yes. He used my easel and created a sketch. The still is of a peach sitting on top of a book. He'd drawn a book before, so I thought it would be easier for him. The peach drawing, although not perfect in balance, is extraordinary in shading. Justin has a gift. His aptitude will far exceed mine and Beck's." She removed the sketch from her portfolio and handed the artistic rendition to the man.

"Good. I knew he'd excel. You'll bring him to class tomorrow?" He all but rubbed his hands together.

Her breath caught. A simple nod had to suffice. Was she making a mistake, getting her son involved in public awareness of his talent?

"I submitted a request to have Justin's work put in the opening of the Longview Art Museum. However--" He shoved his fingers through his gray-black hair. "--Mrs. Hayden Longview has denied the entry unless…"

Shania sat forward and scrubbed her face. Beck's parents could deny Justin's existence as much as they wanted. Why would they reject this one boon and manipulate her life in such a manner? "I'm surprised they recognized his name."

He tilted his chin, obviously shamefaced. "I notified them. Thought they'd want to know."

Bile rose from her stomach, catching in her throat. She picked up her bags. "I've changed my mind. I don't want Justin to be exposed to the propaganda that comes with fame. Thank you, sir, for your attempt."

"Sit down, Miss Miller. They claim the child isn't their son's. The Longviews declared if you won't tell people who you believe Justin's father is and bring along your fiancé they'll allow two pieces of Justin's work in the opening."

"I'd never deny Justin his heritage, especially since Beck doesn't have control over his mental facilities." This entire conversation was ludicrous in nature, and it was unbelievable that the Longviews talked openly with her professor about a personal matter.

"Beck has completely recovered." His keen eyes focused on her.

Her throat felt dry as she forced the vomit down. She hadn't known about Beck's recovery, but she was thankful. Later she'd digest the fact the Longviews felt obligated to deny Justin's relationship to Beck. Had they investigated Justin's birth?

"Who did they say was my fiancé?" Shania's heart pumped as fast as the ten o'clock bells in the tower. She couldn't imagine what they were thinking declaring she was engaged.

He tugged a small yellow sticky-note from his pocket. "Dr. Adam Raimo."

What? How had this happened? What possible benefit would the Longviews get from making her claim she was engaged to Adam? Why would they believe he was her fiancé? Had they been spying on her? The entire situation was too much to bear. She licked her lips and swallowed. "Thank you, Monsieur. If you'll give me Justin's artwork, I'll take it home with me."

Before she took her next breath, Monsieur jumped out of his chair. "No. You can't. His work is groundbreaking. The find alone will be documented in the best, highest-rated art magazines. I'll be famous. Write my ticket to any university I desire. I cannot allow this. I won't let you take the opportunity away from me."

She shook her head, trying to decide what to do. She would reclaim Justin's work and try to get out of this deplorable situation with her grade still intact. "I'm not engaged to Adam. I'll take Justin's work now."

"If I'm able to get Justin's work displayed in another venue, not Longviews', then can I exhibit the sketches?" he insisted.

"I don't think public exposure at age three is a great idea."

His face paled. Was he thinking about the impact his loose tongue had made? He probably thought the Longviews would be rife with gratification to know their grandson possessed such a gift. Why hadn't Monsieur talked to her first?

His eyes narrowed. "I'll try to get his art into another show. If I do, we'll decline Mr. and Mrs. Longviews' very considerate offer. In the meantime I'll contact the Longviews and postpone giving them an answer."

Her stomached stopped its frantic flipping and settled back to normal.

"We have until next Saturday. Do you think you can find a real or *fake* fiancé by then?" His lips tightened into place.

At his announcement her pulse darted to race mode again. He wasn't going to take no for an answer. *No*, her mind screamed. At age twenty-three, she'd never imagined dealing with this type of situation. Her stomach muscles cramped in anxiousness stirring the contents as she contemplated her choices.

She glanced at the clock, ten. She'd miss the last bus to her apartment if she didn't leave now.

"I don't know. No. Probably. I need to leave." She needed to get out. Being coerced wasn't something she enjoyed. She had to consider the facts before she made a decision.

"I'll call the Longviews early tomorrow and ask for a couple of days. I'll let you know what they say after class." He pounded an index finger on his desk, a fast rap.

She nodded and ran out of his office. The white and red stripped bus crept away from the curb. She ran forward, shouting. A sympathetic soul must have asked the driver to stop. Shania jumped on board the second the doors opened. Seated, she slowed her breathing and dropped her head into her hands. Despite the Longviews' urging for her to disappear when she was three months pregnant with their grandchild, they would never stay out of her life. She didn't understand. Beck had been liberated from her. The ring returned. Freedom apparently didn't close a gate to meddling.

"Last stop," the bus driver declared.

She numbly rose from the seat and followed the other passengers off. Her portfolio dragged along the steps as she climbed to the top floor of the apartment building. She leaned her head against the door. No way in. She'd left her key with Morgan.

Like a sledgehammer her hand fell onto the knob. After a slight turn, it rolled and opened. Morgan thought of her. Her true knight--forever?

The desk lamp on the foyer table provided a dim glow. He wasn't sitting on the sofa waiting as she'd expected.

She dropped her bags inside, shut and locked the door. A shrug and her coat fell off, adding to the pile in the mini-foyer. She stepped over the heap and went into the bathroom. Teeth brushed, clothing exchanged for a brown tank top and matching boxers, she shuffled into the bedroom, leaving jeans, top and undergarments on the floor.

Currently, her knight was sprawled on her bed. Justin must have worn him out. Toddlers expelled a great deal of energy and Morgan wasn't use to the pace. She climbed onto the mattress beside Morgan and drew the covers up to her chest. She willed her breathing to slow and the pounding against her ribs stopped.

A glance. Eyes closed, lashes resting on his cheeks were model perfect. The shadow of a beard, slight blond bristles, created an odd tingle down in her belly. In the past a simple gaze from him ignited heat in the space between her thighs.

This would be the first time she'd ever shared a bed with a man for an entire night. What typically happened when a woman woke in bed with a man? With a guy who made her want to sing blissful tunes?

She wouldn't think about his lips. Exhausted in mind and body she tried to relax. She reviewed her conversation with her professor and quickly jumped to her psychology professor's lecture yesterday. He had said, "With all journeys in life, it is necessary to review the past before moving on to the future."

Shania reflected back to that cold October day, four years ago.

* * * *

"Morgan, I need to tell you something important in person and ask you to take me somewhere," she whispered into her parents' landline phone. Bags packed, tears dried, she was prepared to leave. Her parents hadn't accepted her decision to keep the baby. Maybe Beck's family would.

"I'll be there in five." He drove his 4x4 truck onto the brick driveway exactly five minutes later. Shania and Watson--her parents' houseman--stood beside piles of luggage.

Morgan stepped out of the truck. His eyes held a glint of curious fear. He glanced at the bag. The spark changed into anger. "What's going on?"

"Thank you, Watson. Morgan will help me." She shook the man's hand.

"Good luck, Miss Shania," he replied and silently left.

"What happened?" Morgan hugged her. Over the past three months, since Beck deployed, they'd become closer. She appreciated his quiet personality, gentle nature and dependability.

"The short version, I'm pregnant. My parents want me to have an abortion. I refused. Now, I need to find out if Beck's parents will help me." She caught her breath. At nineteen, she had a life growing inside her and the possibility of nowhere to go. Thank goodness for Morgan.

He stepped away and grabbed the two pieces of luggage. "All right. It'll be a two, almost three hour drive. Are you up for it?"

She wiped the tears running down her face. What choice did she have? She cleared her sore throat. "Yes. Thank you, Morgan."

Jaw tight, he gave her a brief smile and nodded. He carried two bags to his truck and hoisted them in the back. He assisted her inside. On the way to Briarwood she explained her parents' reaction. They wanted Beck as a son-in-law and grandchildren, but not in the reverse order, especially not knowing if the child had been fathered by Beck. Shania explained her mother's wish to have her remain pure until marriage. Their lack of trust, disappointment and rejection hurt, deep down, cutting into her core.

Two bathroom stops later they drove near the iron gates of Beck's home. Morgan pressed the monitor button on the security box outside his window.

"Morgan Hardwick and Shania Miller."

"Sure, drive in, Morgan." Mr. Longview's smiling image came onto the screen of the miniature plasma.

"They like you," Shania whispered, holding her hand to her stomach, hoping she wouldn't vomit on their beautiful lawn.

"Beck and I've been friends since freshman orientation." He tapped her black trousers as if to say, "relax."

Her clothes fit tighter. What would she do when she couldn't get into any of her pants?

Beck's parents were very nice to Morgan and pleasant to her. Conversation about Beck and his tour overseas complete, Shania controlled her shaking hands and presented the topic.

"I'm going to be blunt, because it's getting late. I'm pregnant. My parents are not willing to help me, so I'm begging you to please assist me, emotionally and financially. I wouldn't be a bother. I'd stay in Beck's room." She bit her lip and clasped her hands on her lap.

Mr. Longview frowned and got up to get a refill on his drink. Whiskey, by the golden hue of the liquid. The silence was profound. Shania glanced at Morgan to see if he could give her a clue. His face remained impassive.

She knew him well enough by now to recognize his green eyes glittered with anger.

"No, Shania," Mrs. Longview snarled. "You're a Jezebel. I told Beck you'd trap him into marriage. Is that why you became engaged, because you were pregnant?" Mrs. Longview jumped from the sofa. "I saw you coming out of Tom's apartment. Your hair was wet and you were flushed, as if you'd fornicated."

"Whoa. You're going too far with this, Mrs. Longview. I've known Shania for six months or more and I can vouch for her. She doesn't have the character for such a thing. Beck loves her." Morgan stood and held out his hand to Shania.

She used the padded part of the cherry armrests as leverage and rose from the pink striped chaise. Her legs wobbled as the impact of their opinion took root. The Longviews dismissed her. She glanced at the ring representing a promise made by Beck. Had he known his parents weren't in favor of the union?

"We'll deny the child, Miss Miller," Mrs. Longview stated as Morgan grasped Shania's arm. "You will not get any of our money. Thank goodness Beck didn't act rashly and marry you before he left the States."

Tears ran down Shania's face, but she choked back the sobs. She wouldn't allow them to hear her pain. She couldn't ask them for Beck's address, or it'd confirm he didn't care for her. Why hadn't he written?

The maid opened the door. Morgan held tightly onto her arm. She would have fallen if he hadn't. He helped her into his truck and climbed behind the steering wheel. What could he possibly think of her? Tom or Too Many was Morgan's friend. Would Morgan believe the infidelity accusation?

Where would she go? How would she live? She wanted to hide her shame.

Morgan pounded his fist against the steering wheel. "I'm sorry. They were despicable."

She dug through her purse clanking items together to cover her snivels. Out of the corner of her eye, she saw his jaw tightened and a tic appeared below his left cheek. "I didn't do what they said, Morgan."

"I know. Don't worry, I promised Beck I'd take care of you. I'll find someplace for you to stay. I'll help you, Shania."

The sobs broke free. She turned away from Morgan, dragged a tissue from the inside of her bag and stifled the noise. Her stomach vibrated with the agony. She'd always done the right thing. One variation, having sex with a man, her fiancé, had created a vortex. Her parents and her lover's parents abandoned her. Doubted her. Morgan had been her lifesaver.

* * * *

Shivers ran over her body as the horrible memories ended. She turned onto her side. M-two held sentry outside the window of her university apartment bedroom and the real Morgan lightly breathed beside her. She loved him.

Would Morgan be her knight and help her once again?

Chapter 11

Morgan had slept deeply, something he hadn't done in the past four years. Heat radiated his left side and while not uncomfortable, it was unfamiliar. Could Patty have snuck into his bed again? He'd told her to never stay over until they were married. No, they'd separated.

A whiff of vanilla, baby oil and a scent uniquely Shania's flowed under his nose. He must be hallucinating. The desire to have her beside him in bed drove him to smell her, if only he could taste her lips, he'd freely forfeit his mind. He'd masturbated every time he envisioned Shania removing her bridesmaid's dress and running down the hallway. He'd never glimpsed her unclothed body until then--she'd always been an image in a dream. A radiant beauty rested right beside him in bed making him the luckiest damn man on planet Earth.

Morgan opened his eyes to see her lightly breathing, blowing her short light brown locks away from her face. Two months ago her waist-length hair gave the appearance of naivety, like a young and untried Samson. The new short and sassy style emphasized her life's experiences, the battles she'd taken on and won or lost. She'd been an insecure female before and now she was a strong and confident woman and mother.

He glanced at Justin. Through the filmy gauze curtain he could see the little boy, arms flung wide in sleep. Morgan shifted onto his side, reached and pushed the hair behind Shania's ear. She moaned and flopped onto her back. A soft mellow sigh flowed from her perfect lips.

His gaze traveled the length of her body and focused on her delectable breasts. Her tank top had pulled tight against her chest. Her nipples peaked, as if they sensed his desire to taste them.

He inched closer, placing an arm on her other side, and kissed her.

"Morgan," she whispered, making his name sound like a gift granted from the sleep fairy.

A gentle touch to her lips, a light nibble, was what he'd planned, until she murmured his name. Then he wanted everything, to touch her skin and make sweet passionate love with her.

Her amber eyes opened. Their gazes latched. A glimmer of happiness changed to sparkling pleasure. His fingers caressed her face, then he kissed her. Not the gentle nice-to-see-you-Aunt Betty, but a full-force lip locking. His tongue touched hers. Upon the invitation she joined in the thrust and parry game. Too soon, his cock infused with desire and filled his pants. His greatest need was to reach toward her. His hips shifted, giving her space. He took a tense breath. As he slowly exhaled, he weaved his fingers through her hair.

She moved closer and kissed his neck. Breasts larger than his hands pressed tight to his chest. Her palms caressed his back. His hand sinfully touched her firm thigh. He stroked the backside of her knees, then her soft inner skin between her legs. His finger smoothed the groove of her folds and felt the wetness flooding her panties.

"Mommy," Justin said. His voice was close.

Morgan rubbed his forehead against hers, licked her lips tasting her one more time, and flopped back.

Her breath came out in quick burst of air. He closed his eyes, she was as excited about the possibility of them being together as he was.

She inhaled, groaned, and then leaned on her elbow. "Good morning, honey."

"Peaches and crunch cereal?" Justin asked.

Morgan squinted to look at Justin. The child wrapped his hand around his favorite blue blanket. Morgan smiled and patted the covers beside him. Justin climbed up and snuggled. Morgan draped his arm around his son. Shania lay down on his other side. He entwined his fingers with hers. His family. Today, he'd ask Shania to marry him--forever.

"Is that a phone ringing?" Morgan flexed his fingers, not wanting to let her go.

"Yes, mine. It could be my art instructor." She climbed from the bed and ran into the living room. Her tight butt, encased in the soft thin cloth, flashed him.

"I'm hungry," Justin whined.

"Get up and I'll fix you breakfast," Morgan said. Justin continued to remain fitted, like a dovetailed drawer. The kid's stomach growled.

Morgan tickled him until he got off the bed. Jeans tugged into place, Morgan meandered into the living room. Shania talked with a sharp tone into a cellphone. She'd changed, became harder, edgier, in the past three years. She wasn't Samson after all--or was she?

"Why would you tell the Longviews we were engaged?" She finger-combed her hair. "What?"

Morgan stopped washing his hands. His stomach muscles clenched. He reached into a cupboard, removed a bowl and plate sporting cartoon characters on the outside, and dumped organic oat cereal filling the bowl to the top of Diego's head. Grabbing the carton of milk from the fridge, he topped the carbs and glanced at Shania. Her face blanched and her hands shook.

"I'll call you later." She disconnected and placed the phone on the coffee table. "I'll be back in a minute."

Morgan twisted the lip on a jar of peaches and pulled out a few slices with the tips of his fingers. He placed them on the plate. His heart rate escalated, but he refused to show any anxiety. Engaged?

"Where you going?" Justin asked from his child-sized chair positioned at the coffee table.

Shania grabbed her coat, slipped on a pair of flip-flops and left the apartment. Odd behavior.

Justin glanced at Morgan and frowned.

Morgan slipped a spoon into floating O's and placed the bowl and plate beside Justin. "Why don't you wash your hands before you eat?"

"Where'd Mommy go?" He glanced at the door and then met Morgan's stare.

"Not sure, buddy. We'll ask when she returns." Where had she gone, dressed in a lightweight overcoat, on top of her underwear, and flip flops? The predicted temperature was thirty degrees. Whatever she sought must be important, especially since it involved the Longviews and an engagement.

Morgan had put a napkin beside Justin's plate when Shania barreled through the door, slamming it in her wake. She wiggled out of her sandals and shook off the coat, keeping her stare on the article. Morgan craned his neck to see the name of the newspaper, *Briarwood's View*, a student daily.

"What is it?" Morgan asked, walking toward her as she stood holding her coat between two fingers of one hand and crunching the paper with the other.

He took the jacket and secured it to a peg on the rack. He bent to grab her book bag and portfolio. She wouldn't normally drop her stuff, nor stand in a stupor while reading.

Her tiger eyes connected with his glance. Anger and fear radiated from their amber depths.

"Justin, eat your breakfast. Your mom and I want to talk, okay?" Morgan asked.

"TV?"

Morgan looked to Shania for guidance. At one time he knew their routine, but Shania had changed and maybe her habits had as well.

"This one time," she said, her voice resonating like nails scratching sandpaper instead of her usual sexy tone.

Justin grabbed the remote and a few minutes later the sound of a detergent commercial resounded in the room.

Morgan took her arm, leading her into the bedroom. "What's happened?"

She dropped onto the edge of the bed and bit her lip. "Last Friday my drawing professor, Monsieur Barrett, allowed me to take Justin to class. Justin listened to the lecture and drew an amazing sketch."

She grabbed Morgan's hand. "You should see it. His highlighting and shadowing are perfect and instinctive. Monsieur Barrett said Justin was a genius and wanted to get the piece into an art show. The new Longview Art Museum is due to open, and without consulting me, he talked to the Longviews. They were not happy. Monsieur convinced them of the notoriety they could obtain by placing Justin's artwork in the grand opening. They said the work could be entered only if I brought my fiancé along. I don't have a fiancé."

His quick breaths came at a painful rate, making his chest ache. Adam's name came to mind. "You don't?"

"No," she squealed and looked at him as if he had two heads. "But whoever reads the BV will think I do. Look at this."

He took the paper and smoothed out the wrinkles. Right on the center page was a picture of her being given a grossly large diamond ring. Shania was glancing at the other people at the table, Justin and his pediatrician. He read the caption. "Local MD and Briarwood physiology professor, Adam Raimo, proposes to art student, Shania Miller, during dinner at Meat and Boards."

"He hadn't. The show required audience participation. The knight gave me the ring, a token of his affection. An act. A farce." She rubbed the top of her forehead. "I tried to get Justin's artwork back from Barrett. He refuses to release the sketch. He wants to be recognized as the one who discovered an astonishing young artist. Although he claims he'll try to get into another art show, he wants to keep the Longview slot so he can get his name in the press. I'm not sure he'll try very hard because he told me I'm to bring a fiancé, fake or not, to the opening. How do I get out of this situation? What do I do now?"

"Do you care for Raimo?" His mind regretted the question. Blood rushed to his heart and thumped in anticipation. His stomach tightened as he waited for an answer. Morgan hoped she'd tell him she loved him. Hadn't she made that statement at the church a couple of months ago, or had the love announcement, indeed, been a figment of his imagination?

She sighed, as if the weight of her future sat heavy on her shoulders. "He's just a friend."

"I'll be your fiancé." He stood, folded the newspaper and grabbed her hand. "Let me be your intended. Say you'll marry me."

* * * *

Shania gazed into his beautiful green eyes. She should refuse. He'd done enough. She'd destroyed his wedding, and hadn't been in contact with him in two months. Accepting his proposal would be using him. She released his hand. No declaration of love. Did he love her as she loved him?

Shania couldn't respond to his offer because she actually did want to marry him. A fake engagement would be impossible to accept, desiring him the way she did. She certainly didn't want a marriage proposal to be the result of a newspaper article. Minutes ticked by and she needed to get Justin ready for class which started in one hour.

"Why didn't you marry Patty?" she asked. He flinched. She wished she could take the question back. Too soon. They hadn't had a chance to talk. Her life was a huge palette of changing colors, some blending and others in direct contrast. "Never mind. It's none of my business. It's time to get ready for class. I can't imagine what is waiting for me at the end of today's lecture with Monsieur Barrett."

She rose from the bed.

He grabbed her hand. "You were right. Patty and I didn't belong together. She wasn't the person I truly wanted. I guess you don't know someone unless you spend time with them daily. Sometimes even your best friends are false, not truly caring about you or others."

Was he talking about Beck? Shortly after Morgan moved her into the small house, he refused to answer Beck-related questions. While Shania focused on providing a home for her baby, Beck had been taken prisoner. Morgan had finally told her he and Beck weren't friends any longer. His cheek tic indicated he wouldn't say more.

"Thank you for telling me. You hurt me that night, coming to my house. I begged you to kiss me. You didn't tell me you hadn't married Patty. At the church I told you I loved you and later I said I wanted to be with you. You kissed my hair and left."

He lowered his gaze, then wove his fingers with hers and refocused on her face. "I'm sorry. I should have done things differently."

Her throat hurt again, like it had on his supposed wedding night. Why did loving someone hurt so much?

Shania was a stronger woman now. She would not cry.

"I need to go. Are you leaving today?" she whispered. She focused on pleasant thoughts to keep her mind busy. His bare chest flashed before her. He had a perfect muscular body. He'd obviously worked outside without a shirt during the summer. A faint white line separated his sturdy trunk from where his jeans fit loose on his hips. She released his hand, started to place her fingers on his upper torso, but stopped. Her ribs hurt from her breaths pounding against them. She had hoped he would say, "Become my fiancée because I'm in love with you."

"Is your class with the professor who's trying to use you and Justin?" His calm, controlled voice made her quiver. His fists tightened at his sides. Morgan was anything but serene.

"Yes." She grabbed his arm, feeling the muscles tense under her hand. "He's doing what he has to survive in academia. To be honest with you, I was so proud of Justin I wanted Monsieur Barrett to get the artwork into a show."

The warm skin under her fingertips relaxed. He smiled that comfortable easy-going smile she was used to seeing.

"I have to work this weekend, but I'd like to walk you to class. Justin and I'll get juice and coffee while we're waiting for you. I'll leave after we talk."

"Sounds great. I'll get ready." She released his arm. Now, what to wear and how to counter whatever comments resulted from the newspaper article? Should she accept Morgan's offer to be her fake fiancé?

His jaw tightened. "I'll be having a word with Monsieur Barrett."

* * * *

Morgan glanced at Justin who rocked from heel to toe making the green and yellow lights flash on the shoes. Morgan tried to wipe his mind of the red tint that'd flowed over Shania's face when she'd seen the purchase. Tight funds? He hadn't wanted to embarrass her, so he claimed the footwear was an early Christmas present.

He anticipated her commenting on the food, but she hadn't. He figured her mind was centered on her predicament. Morgan had every intention of ending that ruse. The entire article could be a mistake. However what was the likelihood that the week before finals, a university student photographer happened to be at a restaurant catering to Briarwood community?

No, the good doctor had arranged the story. Adam Raimo wanted Shania. He wasn't getting her. She belonged to Morgan, and he would not give her up again. He should have fought for her initially, should have acted that first day they'd met. Beck had arrived at their apartment infatuated with Shania's sexy body and beautiful face. Morgan went to meet the paragon a few hours later at the student union. At the sight of her, his pectoralis muscles expanded, the fan-like structure jerked, rattling his ribcage. Later he fell in love with her innocent nature, sensitivity, joy of life and connection to art. He was surprised to learn she was from his hometown of Cyan, Indiana. If he recalled correctly, his father had mentioned Mr. Miller had political ambitions.

Her father's and Beck's minds had run along the same track. Both wanted to advance in politics. Beck chose to go into the military, not out of loyalty to his country, but to further his stately goals to become governor of the State of Indiana. Mr. Longview had received assurances Beck wouldn't be under fire. None of those promises were known by the rebels who snatched him off the city streets in Iraq.

As promised, Morgan took care of Shania, falling deeper in love as time passed. He had numerous opportunities to declare his feelings, but he couldn't. No, the truth was he wouldn't because Beck had been his friend. However, any occasion Morgan could get to spend time with Shania, he took.

Even when his world came crashing to a halt. He stared at the white hallway wall and reflected to the day Beck announced he was going to marry Taffy Canterbury, who sported a larger, more brilliant diamond than Shania did. Morgan ended the friendship with Beck the day he found out. Not wanting to end his relationship with Shania, he helped her decorate the little house and went to Lamaze classes with her. Beck's capture by rebels and subsequent PTSD interrupted Morgan's plans. Finally Morgan realized Shania held onto the hope she and Beck would reunite, and Morgan had to come to terms with that.

He grieved, then decided to get on with life. Too Many introduced him to Patty Tancor. She was cute, saucy--the opposite of calm, beautiful

Shania--and just what he needed to ease suffering. Until that fateful day when Shania came to the church.

"Hi, Justin," a baritone voice quaked.

Morgan came out of his reverie and glanced at Dr. Adam Raimo. The closer he got, the faster Morgan's mind raced with accusations.

"Hi," Justin timidly responded and grabbed Morgan's hand.

"Hi, I'm Dr. Adam Raimo. You're ah...Shania's friend..." Raimo pinched his chin between two fingers as if in thought.

Morgan offered a hand. "Morgan Hardwick."

Adam gave him a sharp, tight handshake. Morgan wasn't intimidated, although his stomach tightened in preparation for a confrontation.

Much to Morgan's dismay the door to the classroom opened, sending students forth and interrupting his conversation with Raimo. A few choice words pounded his mind. He would share them with the good doctor another time and place.

Shania didn't appear. Morgan held Justin's hand, and they walked into the classroom. Empty. He heard her voice, raised in anger. The breathing on his neck meant Raimo was hot on his heels.

Justin broke free, running around easels to an open doorway. Morgan put space between him and Hot Breath, easing into the office after Justin. Before he could introduce himself, or even make eye contact with Shania, the less-than-honest professor said, "Ah, you must be the fiancé. I'm Monsieur Barrett."

"What?" Raimo protested. A heavy silence fell over the office. Morgan glanced at Shania and the look held.

"Awkward," Monsieur Barrett stated, without the French accent, as he glanced between Morgan and Raimo.

Shania fell onto a hard wooden chair, her bag plopping in front of her. Justin ran to her side, and placed a small hand on her jean-clad thigh.

Morgan wasn't a man to sit on his laurels. The professor was referring to Raimo as the fiancé, but Morgan would take advantage of the misconception.

"Raimo, you didn't know? Shania and I are engaged, as of last night." Morgan smiled broadly.

"You didn't get married, Hardwick?" Raimo narrowed his eyes.

The asshole wouldn't win. As far as Morgan was concerned the engagement wasn't fake, and he had every intention of making her Mrs. Morgan Hardwick.

"No, I couldn't let the love of my life get away, so here I am." Morgan laughed, in his head at least. His chest might have puffed out, because he enjoyed Raimo's uneasiness.

"Three months later?" Raimo expounded, taking a step closer to Morgan.

Morgan raised a hand, palm out.

Shania rubbed her forehead. "The time doesn't matter. I realize the Longviews could have mistaken we were engaged, Adam, from the newspaper article. I think it'd be silly to ask for a retraction, unless you'd like to do so?"

The ten week, two day, thirteen hour gap from the canceled wedding to now was an issue that Morgan needed to address with Shania. Had she mentioned his absence to Raimo? He glanced at her. She bit her lip. Morgan knew she hated conflict. Confrontation made her nauseous. It took a great deal of courage for her to face Barrett, and now Raimo.

"Not necessary. Maybe I'll be the most sought after bachelor if people find out you aren't going to be my wife." Raimo jeered and then glared at her.

Shania paled and grabbed the arms of the chair. The dig could only be a reference to Beck's wedding announcement and his past rejection of Shania. The man needed a good beating.

"Dr. Raimo, I'd like to talk to you in private. Outside." Morgan nodded. His jaw hurt from clenching his teeth.

"No!" Shania shouted and then whispered, "Please, I just want this to be over. Adam, I'm sorry if you've been hurt. I meant no offense. I apologize for my gruff manner on the phone this morning." She reached out to him. "The most valuable lesson I've learned the last three years is how important friends are, sometimes more vital than family. I want to be your friend. Please, let's be friends."

Dr. Raimo gave a sharp nod, pivoted and left the room at breakneck pace.

Shania straightened her shoulders. "Monsieur Barrett, I do not intend to have Justin's work shown at the art museum. If you can find a new show, one not associated to the Longviews, you have permission to enter them. If not, then I'll be reclaiming the pieces."

She stood, hoisted her bags onto her shoulder, and took Justin's hand into hers. "Come along, honey."

She held out her other palm to Morgan.

He entwined his fingers with hers. His gaze met hers. Crazy wonderful ecstasy overwhelmed him, making his pulse go berserk.

"Have time for lunch?" Morgan asked. They walked out of the building and into the sunlight.

"Yes, this is my last class until a final next Wednesday," she admitted.

"Terrific. Will you come back to Cyan with me?"

Chapter 12

Shania stood in front of the French door, letting a bit of fresh crisp fall air into Morgan's house. The slight breeze refreshed her. A large window framed the lakefront, which glowed in its picturesque beauty several yards away. Muted greens, golds and blues created a colorful Monet look-a-like. The squawking voices of Canadian geese pierced through the portal.

She glanced at Justin, sprawled on the chocolate brown sectional sofa, his breath lightly blowing the fur on his toy horse. Birds honking hadn't woken him. The grilled chicken and mac and cheese he'd eaten for lunch must have set heavy in his stomach.

The thump of plastic hitting tile brought her around. Their limited luggage sat in the middle of the foyer. She smiled and whispered, "Thank you for unloading our car. Did I park over far enough so you could get out if you need to go somewhere?"

"You're fine. I'll take your Jeep tomorrow and fill it with gas. You'll have a full tank to go back on Wednesday." Morgan joined her at the open door and held her in a loose hug.

She met his stare. "I'm glad you didn't sell your house. I think it's lovely."

"I agree. Selling the cottage and marrying Patty would have been a mistake." He wove his fingers through her short locks. "Why did you cut your hair so short? You look like Tinker Bell."

She tried to pull away. He held tight. "I hadn't heard from you in two months and assumed our friendship was at an end. I needed to start fresh. A new look, a new attitude, and new goals."

Morgan kissed her, much like he had this morning when they awoke. Passionate. Hot. And totally immersing her into a tightly strung tethered web of lust. He broke the connection and trailed his lips to her ear. "I'm sorry, let me explain."

His voice held a hint of regret woven through it. She wanted to hear his explanation, although his kiss sent tingles into her stomach. The space between her thighs ached with desire. Her hips gravitated toward him, despite her mind reminding her sex equaled pain. He kissed the side of her cheek.

Shania put distance between them. After a pause, she pivoted to gently close the French door. "Please do."

"At the church, you told me you loved me." He paused. "Do you love me, Shania?"

Her breath caught in her throat. What was he leading up too? Did he love her and was ready to announce it? "Yes, I'll love you forever, Morgan."

He jerked, but his face lit with a wave of elation. "That day, I told Patty I wasn't marrying her. I think I accepted her proposal because I wanted something. Something I didn't believe I'd ever be able to have and to hold. Something I might have a chance of obtaining now." He closed the distance between them and placed his hands on the sides of her face. His lips touching hers, soft and searching, made her want to weep with happiness.

She moaned and settled her hands on his muscular broad shoulders. Well-built biceps pushed tight against his cotton shirt. Her fingers moved to his narrow waist, then rested on his perfectly shaped firm rear. A bum she'd admired on many occasions.

"Why did you take so long to find us?" she dogged. She needed to know why he delayed talking to them, seeing them, wanting them. From his words, he didn't truly care for Patty, did he? What did he mean, "obtaining now"? Could that illusive need be love? Was his proposal for real?

He grimaced. "I couldn't come to you until I had Patty taken care of, the mess resolved. I was working three jobs. If I called you, talked to you, the moment I heard your voice I'd have dropped my obligations and flown to be by your side. Unencumbered or not. Each of those days we were apart I thought of nothing but you and Justin. I'd fall into bed each night with your image in my mind. I wanted you--want you--so much, I knew I couldn't see or talk to you unless we could be together," he confessed. "I hope you still want me, because I need you in my life."

Oh God, his words were sweet. "Morgan." Her breath caught.

Morgan would always remain true to his character. Honest, loyal and straightforward. She took his hand into hers and pulled him down the hallway to his bedroom. The fear of pain during intercourse made her stomach muscles jump, as if overworked with crunches. She didn't know why he needed to work two or three jobs, but his voice was filled with love. Everything bad disappeared. His kisses made her clit ache and her breasts feel heavy. His touch sent her nerve endings into a tailspin. You can do this, she told herself.

He slid his arm around her waist. She turned into him, bumping their bodies together. Her nipples peaked. His mouth lowered to her ear. "You smell fantastic. Flowers and spice."

"And you smell like Morgan." She'd kept one of his white t-shirts. At a painfully lonely time she'd pull the cloth from her bottom drawer and smell it. The real scent was so much better. She put the fear of pain aside and focused on how his touches made her skin come alive. He was the man she'd fallen in love with. Inside his bedroom, he shut the door. She shucked her shoes and socks and unfastened her wool slacks. A quick flick of her fingers and the buttons on her blouse fell out of the holes. She reached for the bottom pearl disc on her top. He held her hand.

"Slow down. I'm pleased you want to be with me, but let's enjoy our first time at making love." He lowered her shaking fingers from the button. The sides of the blue and green polka-dot blouse flopped open. "I like the lacey green bra."

His fingers dragged along her stomach, igniting an internal fire.

"I'm nervous—I don't have a lot of experience." She wished her voice would have rushed from her throat come-sexy instead of tease-weak.

"All the more reason for us to ease into this instead of rushing." He trailed his fingers down her front, touching the crest of one of her breasts then farther down, making her muscles contract with the light caress. "I want you to remember our first time, one of a million times we'll make love, as the best you've ever experienced."

The best, she thought, not that difficult, considering her previous two sexual encounters were excruciatingly painful and marked as hurried. Although sex-talk skills, she had in abundance. "Me too." She touched her lips to his, a light caress.

"Touch me," he whispered.

She lifted the edge of his sweater, stroking her fingers along his smooth hard planes. Sudden desire to taste him, all of him, overwhelmed her. A quick jerk and the material went over his head. He lifted his arms, struggling to get out of the garment. He sucked in his breath when her lips met his skin. Power as she'd never experienced before rushed through her. She'd never been the one to initiate or control the foreplay. Then her insecurities came to the forefront. Was she doing everything correctly?

Her hand lowered to his jeans and sang, "Your cock is so large, I want to touch, touch, touch it."

She unfastened his belt and unzipped, touching the head of his penis through his underwear.

"Shh. You don't have to say things like that to me. It's just us. Be yourself." His hands shot to her waist, to hold her back or pull her forward she didn't know. Even embarrassed about his comment, she knew one thing--she wanted to touch and feel every inch of his well-formed body. A smile spread across her face, he wanted to be with her just as she was. His breathing became labored. Slow and easy, her fingers reached inside the waistband and lowered the pants over his hips. Her mouth touched his nipple as she bent her head to see what existed under the rough material. A deep, pain-filled groan came from his lips.

She glanced at his face. No pain flashed across his face. Her mouth on his skin brought a moan from him, a pleasurable noise. Joy rushed through her, exciting her more than his kisses ever could. Placing her palms against his waist, she slid her anxious fingers under the band of his tight cotton boxers and eased off the only barrier between her hand and his massive organ. His bare chest and taut stomach begged to be savored. As he bent to remove the underwear, her face leveled with his cock. Her lips circled an inch below his belly button and then slipped onto the head, learning the curves and valleys.

Christ, his tool was enormous, massive compared to Beck's. Could she handle twice as much penis stretching her in half? She stopped her explorations and stood upright. Morgan stared at her, not questioning, not judging, and simply being the kind person he was. Rough, callused palms cupped her face and he kissed her. Heated passion rocked her. She opened her lips to accept him. His tongue entered her mouth, nudging hers.

She flicked her tongue between his teeth, flowing over and under his. She nuzzled his lips, outlining their shape. Breaking the contact, she finger-combed his hair, then rested her hands on his hips. He slipped the blouse from her shoulders. The soft cotton fell down to her wrists. A jerk and one sleeve slithered to the side. His fingers unclasped her bra. A second later it disappeared. The blouse quickly followed. Her breasts chilled. Whimpers came from her throat. She needed to feel his skin and to be touched by him.

"Shh, relax. I promised to take care of you. Let me." He lifted her into his arms.

As she longed to do for the past several hours, she placed her fingers on his chest, caressing the tight muscles, stroking up to his neck. A tug and he drew closer to her.

He gave her a smile and an intense powerful stare held as he laid her on the soft comforter. She placed her hands on her nipples, covering them and providing warmth.

Naked, he climbed on the bed. "You're beautiful."

An urgent need rippled through her, she wanted more.

"I think we should have an equal playing field, don't you?" he whispered.

She didn't understand what exactly was happening to her insides, but her fast-paced heartbeat created breathlessness. He nodded to her waist. She lifted off the mattress. His nimble fingers released the latch on her wool slacks, the unzipping adding cadence to their puffs of air. His hand slid through the small opening and touched her backside. In a flash her pants were down around her ankles, and in a whoosh the garment left her body. Every square inch of her skin was caressed as he slowly made his way back to her stomach.

His fingers plucked at one of the tiny bows holding her green underpants together. The ribbon separated and the cloth fell to the side. She rolled, slow, trying to utilize every upper body muscle. He painstakingly unknotted the other tie. Fancy undergarments were her weakness. The panties freed, he removed the material. Nothing existed between them except air and time.

Her skin heated as his tongue wrapped around first one nipple then the other. Tiny fires ignited everywhere. His fingers stroked. Gentle caressing. She oscillated and moaned. The intense pressure became unbearable. How could her body crave to ease the ache between her thighs, knowing the pain was coming? But she did want him. Fear was shoved to the back of her mind. Desire and need took over. She became a free spirit wanting his massive cock to enter her.

She touched his face, wanting to convey her thoughts. He stared at her. Her lips latched onto his mouth. Hot. Those tiny fires merged, heating her limbs to inferno levels. Her hips pressed against his. He broke the kiss then trailed his lips down her side. He spread her thighs and inserted a finger or more into her vagina. His mouth touched her inner thigh skin, kissing his way to her clit. Skyrocketing off the bed, she gasped. He held her hips. Caressing her soft skin, he murmured calming words, creating a new desire.

"What are you doing?" she whispered and lowered her hips to the bed.

"Making love to you. You've never been eat...er...touched in this way?" He held her thighs, refocused his attention and continued to kiss her inner thigh, blowing on her private area.

"No," she gasped.

"Relax. If you don't like what happens, I'll stop." His tongue flicked.

She moaned and pressed against the bed. Her arms lifted, trying to clutch a grounding point, a center of gravity. At a loss, she grabbed the dark blue comforter instead. His strong firm legs rubbed against hers. A mad rush heated her, exploding into a vortex of white fire. Sucked into the tri-fold assault of mind, body and spirit, her senses overwhelmed her. She rocked, digging her heels into the mattress.

"Please help me," she stammered.

He wiped his mouth with the sheet and settled on top of her. Lips nibbled on her neck as his cock found her swollen throbbing entrance. She vibrated with the longing for fulfillment.

His fingers entwined with hers as he kissed her. He slid inside. She expanded. No pain. The urge to move remained strong. She stirred. He moaned, lowering his other hand beside her left shoulder.

He thrust, dipping deep into her sex. She gripped his rear and met his driving force. Their bodies became sweaty as their skin slapped in the ebb and flow of their bump and grind. Her breath became ragged, getting near the end, hoping to find that need to release. Would she die?

She'd never experienced this thrill, this desire to hold a man inside her. She clamped her muscles tight. He hissed, and then groaned. They merged, and like the colors on a palette, blended to create a beautiful loving sexual union.

His seed heated her core as their ragged breathing slowed to normal. She wanted to scream in ecstasy and in horror.

They'd failed to use a condom. Damn, she knew from her mother's lectures, reading material at the free clinic, and her own experience. There was no doubt it took only one time of unprotected sex to create a life.

A fear of the truth squirmed in the back of her mind. She wanted to get pregnant and that's why she hadn't mentioned a condom. There had been plenty of opportunity to slide one on. She knew his character. Morgan would ask her to marry him--for real. He'd want to tie the knot the minute he found out she was with child, but would she feel good about the reason for the marriage?

No. If she were lucky she wouldn't get pregnant. Tomorrow, she'd go to the bank and cash out the CD. She'd pick up some condoms and always, always use them.

Morgan pulled out. Holding the weight of his body off hers, he kissed her and then dropped to her side. "Shania, I want--"

The landline telephone rang. Simultaneously, his watch alarm chimed. "Damn, I forgot." He snatched the phone off the deck and sat on the side of the bed. "Yeah. Sorry, lost track of time. I'll be there in twenty."

He placed the unit on the table and gazed at her. A sheet partially covered his lap. He looked …happy. His smile created new warmth in her, a glow from deep within. She did that, put that look of elation on his face.

"I have to go to work. I promised or I wouldn't leave. I'll return around nine or ten." His voice held an exuberant joyful rhythm.

"I understand. Justin's probably awake. I'll go get him." She slid off the bed, afraid to glance at the sheets. Had blood stained his blue linens?

"I'll shower." He hugged her and walked into the bathroom.

When water splashed in the bath, she leaned across the bed and shoved the cotton aside. Nothing. No spots. No blood. She twisted her leg to look deep on the thigh. Semen. No pink or red substance. What did that mean?

Shania slipped on Morgan's polo and went into the guest bath. Finding a washcloth under the cabinet, she cleaned off and then wrapped a towel around herself, knotting it at her breasts. She went into the master bedroom and laid his shirt across the arm of a hard ladder-back chair. The splashing of water continued. She pulled on her jeans and top. As she buttoned, she considered what the lack of tinted residue meant. Her hand on the doorknob, she stilled and glanced toward the bathroom. Realization came to her, true love paved the way for a painless and blood-free lovemaking session.

Chapter 13

"I'd like to get a payout for a CD that matures today, under the name Shania Anne Miller." Shania tugged Justin's hand, hoping he'd realize kicking the bank teller's wall to make his shoes light up was a bad thing.

"I need to see your driver's license and another form of ID." The gray-haired woman fitted her black rimmed glasses higher on her nose, causing the frame holder chain to jingle. She glanced at Justin and smiled. Apparently she didn't feel the vibrations as his toe connected with the fabric-encased ply-board.

Shania dug out her state license and Briarwood University ID, and slid them across the smooth surface. She needed cash. Justin needed a winter coat. Morgan had purchased shoes for Justin, but she wanted to get him a pair of snow boots. Above all, she'd planned to monitor her money better this quarter.

The bank teller evaluated the identifications with precision. Shania held her breath. Although she was from Cyan and had been a member of this particular branch for the past ten years, she didn't recognize the cashier.

The cash would be used for meals, food, books, tuition and travel back to Briarwood. She touched her short hair. Could she look that different from a year ago when the photos were taken?

"Just a moment, Miss Miller." She wrinkled her nose and slid off her stool, then sashayed to a desk near the back wall.

Relieved, Shania wrapped her arm around Justin's shoulder and whispered in his ear, "Stop hitting your shoe against the wall. It's not nice to kick other people's property. When we're done here, I'll take you to the park. You can knock around a ball or jump on the pavement. Please don't kick anything else."

"Here you go, Miss Miller." The teller was back with a handful of cash and a few pieces of paper. "Let me count it out and then you can sign your name and be on your way." She winked. "It looks like the little guy is anxious to be out in this sun. Snow is expected later today."

The amount was correct. Shania signed her name. "I'd like to deposit half of this into my checking account please." She counted half the cash. "Yes, Justin likes to play in the snow. How much is expected?"

"Just a sprinkle, not enough to build a fort." The teller smiled.

The clerk wrote out a deposit slip. Shania signed the piece of paper and shoved the original and the currency to the woman. She confirmed the amount. Shania stuffed the other half into her wallet. The money deposited, she pushed her printed copy of the receipts into her purse and turned to leave.

She glanced back. "Thank you."

And bumped into a solid wall of flesh. Shania bounced back, almost tripping over Justin. He slid to the side. A hand snatched her arm, preventing her from toppling over. Upright and steady, she glanced at her rescuer. Beck held her in his thin-fingered grasp. Too Many stood at his side.

"Beck," she mumbled. He hadn't released her arm. She shook his fingers loose and stepped away. "Hello, Too Many."

Tom, or Too Many, had football player shoulders and bright blond hair. His shirt sleeves always fit snug against his upper arms, making him appear to be dressed in too small clothing. In contrast to Beck's frown, Too Many had a smile and a glint in his eyes as if barely restraining laughter.

Justin took her hand into his.

"Shania," Beck replied and glanced at Justin.

Justin set one foot on top of the other making the light flash.

"And who is this miniature man?" Beck queried. His knees crackled as he crouched.

Anger rifled through her. Beck, a drug inundated ex-military officer, at first glance might not recognize his son, but he'd been staring for over a minute. Now he lowered to be nose to nose with his mini-me. He'd surely identify an image of his own face. Beck's questioning gaze made contact with hers. She snapped her teeth together. The click of enamel hitting enamel vibrated through her eardrums.

Justin slid behind her leg.

"Beck, you remember meeting Shania's son, Justin, before." Too Many tugged on Beck's arm. He hadn't met Justin. Was Too Many providing a reason to excuse Beck's ignorance?

A confused expression rippled over his eyes. He glanced at Justin and frowned. "Sorry, I guess not."

Shania pulled Justin to stand in front of her, between her legs. "Justin, I'd like you to meet friends of Mommy's, Beck Longview and Tom Moran. Beck and Tom, this is my son, Justin Miller. Soon to be Justin Hardwick."

The lie came swiftly to her lips. She justified her statement telling herself that if Morgan would fall in love with her, he'd marry her and adopt Justin.

Beck jerked as if punched in the face. Too Many snickered, possibly to make Beck feel better or because he recognized her sinful motive. Her good sense had apparently remained in Briarwood and her evil-irrational-self stood in front of, and antagonized, the sperm donor for her child. She wanted Beck to regret denying her and her son. At the very least he could acknowledge their past.

Suspicion set in and being a wicked woman she questioned why they'd come to Cyan. Neither Beck nor Too Many were from the area. Both of their families lived in the outer privileged region of Briarwood. "Why are you in Cyan?"

"I'm dating…a woman from Cyan. We're here for the weekend." Too Many shoved his hands into his pockets and stepped side to side. "Not Beck, he's going back to Briarwood tonight."

Too Many nodded to the gray-haired teller. "We needed some cash."

Shania's glance shot to Beck. A tic vibrated in his jaw and his eyes narrowed. Was he irritated about Justin? Of the handful of times she'd seen Beck in the past year, he'd said no more than twenty words to her. What gave him the right to be angry? Her fear turned into rage, creating a fire in her belly and making her heart pound against her chest. Her knees weakened. She had to get out of there.

Beck's malevolence crept into her blood, freezing her lungs forcing tiny breaths instead of full-bodied puffs.

Justin grabbed the edge of her fall jacket and gave a sharp tug. She hoisted him to rest on her hip. "I hope you have a nice weekend."

She forced her drooping shoulders upright, raised her chin a notch and strode forward. The sensor of the door picked up her emotionally chilled existence and opened. She carried her son into the future, leaving the past behind.

* * * *

Shania purchased a red rubber ball and a few other cosmetic items, and drove to the park. Despite the shining sun, the air was crisp and the play area had very few children. She tossed the orb to Justin and he kicked it a few times, making the monkey bars his soccer goal. He slid down the aluminum slide. She stood within reach in case he toppled.

Justin ran out of energy around noon. She took him to a family-oriented restaurant where children were able to sit in artificial trucks or princess cars to eat a semi-healthy meal. Using the photo feature of her cellphone, she captured his bright smile as he turned the wheel of the pretend vehicle. Later she'd get it printed, and they could hang it beside his bed.

En route to Morgan's house, Justin quietly fell into a light sleep. She parked in the driveway and carried him into the house. After tucking him into the pullout bed, she retrieved her purchases from the car. Back inside she checked the front door to make sure it was locked. She got a bottle of water out of the fridge and leaving her coat on walked outside. A pair of Adirondack chairs with a table separating them had been placed near an oak tree at the pond's edge. The wind cutting across the water's surface chilled the air. Her fingers clasped the zipper to close her jacket. She moved the chair, allowing her to see the house and the lake.

Her mind replayed the day she tried to tell Beck they'd had a son. Shania had left Justin with a neighbor and rushed to Beck's side the minute he arrived at his parents' house in Briarwood. Shivers ran across her skin as she recalled his blank stare. His overly bright eyes did not show emotion. He did not seem to recognize her, as if his vibrant outgoing personality had been sucked out.

* * * *

The Longviews' family physician, Dr. Good, examined Beck. It was only Shania's incredible timing allowed her to hear Dr. Good's explanation about Beck's condition. Otherwise, she would have been left out. Beck's father, John, his mother, Tiffany, and his brother and sister were present. Although the family members were cordial, Shania feared being sent away so she kept quiet.

"A textbook explanation is that Posttraumatic Stress Disorder--PTSD-- is a disorder that can occur after you have been through a traumatic event. During this type of crisis, you think that your life or others' lives are in danger. You may feel afraid or believe that you have no control over what is happening." Dr. Good took a sip of his glass of water.

"Because the human mind continues to be a mystery, recovery time cannot be determined. His recuperation is based on the intensity of the trauma. He can cope. We'll get him treatment, and he can return to his everyday activities, work and relationships. However..." He glanced at

Shania. She tightened her grip on the hard arm of the Queen Anne chair. Why did he look at her?

"We'll get a nurse, a physical therapist to take care of him." Dr. Good glanced at each of them. "In order to recover he will need to avoid triggers that will cause flashbacks, but they can occur without any warning or provocation. Gunfire is the obvious. We'll have to find out if other sights or sounds will cause a relapse."

Shania crossed her legs and tucked her hands under her arms as he pierced her with a black-eyed stare. "Hyperarousal is another symptom we want to avoid. Miss Miller, when or if you visit Beck you'll need to be on guard to not cause him to become angry or irritable. He'll have trouble concentrating and may act out."

She nodded. Why would he address her specifically? The good doctor had obviously been informed of Shania and her claim on Beck.

"Dr. Good, I've read that people with Traumatic Brain Injury might not have positive or loving feelings toward people, especially from his past. He may forget parts of an earlier period because of the painful event. Is this true?" Mrs. Longview raised her tone at the end of the sentence, but her eyes never left Shania.

"Yes, that's true. Beck will have feelings of hopelessness and despair. Of course he'll get consistent counseling, but family members should reassure him. Cognitive-behavioral therapy has proven to help. Generally, for PTSD, eye movement desensitization and reprocessing has recently been incorporated, but often we've found it's not effective for military or combat related cases. Of course, antidepressants are valuable." He finished his glass of water. "Do you have any questions?"

As the queries were voiced Shania listened without comment. She was the interloper, an outsider.

Beck's mother dictated Shania could visit him for one hour the third Monday of each month. Mrs. Longview had more than likely anticipated that the six hours of driving time would deter Shania from seeing Beck. She hadn't expected Shania's determination and loyalty. She had made a promise to Beck before he left for Iraq and she'd honor it, although her emotions became turbulent and confused when he hadn't recognized her.

The first month, Beck had remained in silent stupor. She had kissed him and stayed the entire allotted time, holding his hand.

The next month, he was in the solarium. She greeted him with a kiss.

"Don't," Beck said.

"What?"

"Don't put your mouth on mine," he demanded.

Hurt, she shook off the pain and glanced at his caregiver. Beck's young nurse, dressed in jeans and a form fitting top, always hovered nearby.

Shania showed Beck a recent photo of Justin she'd had taken a few weeks before at Memories, a Cyan photography studio.

Beck gave her a blank eyed stare and returned his gaze to the nurse.

"That's not my son." His robotic answer pierced her heart.

Shania sniffed back the tears, packed her bag of mementoes, and left him. She'd failed. She couldn't remind him or bring the love they once shared fresh to his mind. Downtrodden, she returned to Cyan.

The following month she approached him with the intent to end their farce of an engagement. The maid showed her to the bright sun-filled conservatory. Beck's usual daze seemed less invasive. He smiled, acting as though he was happy to see an old friend.

She placed her bag beside his chair and kissed his thin cheek, as he preferred. His nurse wore a sexy white dress. Oddly enough, jealously didn't wiggle into Shania's system. She smiled and sat in the chair nearest Beck.

"How are you today?"

"Great. Feeling just great." He watched the nurse bend to place an exercise mat on the floor.

"Do you remember who I am?" Shania asked.

"Of course. You're a friend from my past." He didn't look at her.

"No. Do you know how we're connected, how we know each other?" She touched his arm.

He glanced at her fingertips on his wrist and then into her eyes. "You're Miss Miller from Cyan."

She hated that he called her Miss Miller.

"Yes, you're right, Beck." She blinked back tears.

He turned away. "Miss Miller?"

"Yes, Beck," she whispered. He glanced at her again, staring through her.

"Before I forget, my mother said to ask you for the ring. Do you know what she's talking about?" His unemotional tone matched his quick change from nurse-interest lust to cold lifeless eyes.

She glanced at the engagement ring decorating her finger. Not once had she removed it, not even during the bloated days of her last month of pregnancy.

Weights clanged together behind her. Beck's physical therapy session followed her visit. She bowed her head and used the sleeve of her twin-set to wipe her eyes. Their time together had ended. A gripping pain squeezed her stomach, and her tongue felt swollen.

The skimpily dressed nurse slithered in front of Beck, five pound weights clutched in her hand. Beck's glance followed the woman.

"Would you excuse us a moment?" Shania asked her.

"I'm not to leave his side, especially when you visit." A shadow of sympathy crossed over her dark eyes.

How insulting. Yet again, validation that Mrs. Longview would never have accepted Shania into their family. "Please, today will be the last time I'll ever see him."

She nodded, set the weights on the exercise mat and shuffled through the French doors to the outdoor garden. Beck continued to watch her beautiful sway.

Shania dropped to the floor in front of his chair and placed her hands on his knees. "Beck." Her voice came out throaty.

His gaze shot to her face, his eyes searching hers. A memory had sparked, she was sure of it.

"I do understand how your life seems out of your control. For the past three years I've experienced a similar condition as I waited for you and hoped you'd return to me."

"I'm here now." He sounded like his old self.

"Not just physically return to me, but mentally as well. I'd hoped we could become a family, you, Justin and me." Her fingers shook as she removed the ring from her left hand and placed the insignificant token on his lap. "I know that's never going to happen. You may never remember me, which makes me so very sad."

"I'm sorry," came his cheerless reply.

"Goodbye." She broke the rule and kissed his cold lips. "Peace be with you."

* * * *

Until today, that was the last time Shania had seen Beck Longview. The squawk of ducks grounded her into the present. Chilled, Shania shook off the memory. She grabbed her untouched bottle of water and reentered the house. With cold stiff fingers, she reached into her backpack, removed her books and settled onto the sofa. Today was a new day for her, and the past would remain lost. She had the love of a good man and a future with him.

Justin woke from his nap. She arranged apple slices and peanut butter with a sippy-cup on a bed tray. He enjoyed the snack as he watched a Discovery Channel program about whales.

Shania tried to focus on the marketing text, trying to commit the information to memory, with little success. Although business courses were an option, she wanted to know how to run her own art studio if the occasion would present itself. She looked as the kitchen door opened and Morgan stood in the afternoon light.

* * * *

Morgan removed his coat and hung it on the hall tree. He sucked in his stomach and walked forward, inches from her beautiful face.

"How's the studying going?" he whispered into her ear. Her scent excited him. He didn't think he'd have the chance to smell, touch and love her. The mix of aromas of her womanly fragrance and the bottled perfume reminded him of last night and the awesome sex they'd shared. "You smell delicious."

"This text is mind-numbing, and thank you," she replied and kissed his cheek.

He threw his suit jacket over the back of the sofa, and then came around to sit beside her. She marked the page with her stack of notes. He glanced at the title, *Sketching and Drawing: The First Steps for the Professional Artist* by Monsieur François Barrett. The man was certainly an egoist, making his students buy his manuscript. Instant book sales for the professor. She placed the hardback on the sofa.

Morgan wrapped his arm around her. He took her lips in a gentle kiss. She ignited, and he wanted to capitalize on her excitement. A moan escaped him as he drew in air. God, how he wanted her.

"Daddy, play ball?" Justin stammered, touching Morgan's knee with his small hand.

Morgan broke the kiss and glanced at Justin. "Sure, buddy, I'll change clothes and we'll go outside. Maybe when we come in I'll be able to eat whatever has that yummy smell?"

He referred to the roast aroma coming from the kitchen, although the double entendre wasn't missed by Shania. A beautiful color of red highlighted her strong cheekbones. Her fingers trembled as she smoothed tiny locks of hair behind her ear.

Morgan gave her a light kiss. He rose from the sofa, grabbed Justin and tickled his sides. "Go put on your coat and gloves. Maybe your mom can get some bread crumbs, and we'll feed those hungry geese."

"Do you have to work tonight?" Shania made her way into the kitchen.

Morgan had modernized the cottage by removing walls and installing an updated kitchen. The new space was wider and with a woman's touch it could be homey.

"For a few hours, I need to leave at seven. I'll try to be back around ten." He lifted his jacket from the sofa, appreciating the sense of family created by Shania and Justin being with him. "My parents would like us to join them for dinner tomorrow night at their house. Will you go with me?"

"Sure, I like your parents and love the warmth of their farm house." She removed a few slices of bread, the heels and a few others from the end.

Justin ran to her, holding the two pieces of his coat's zipper together.

"Great, I'll let them know." His parents couldn't wait to welcome Shania and Justin into their family. Morgan ambled down the hallway to the master bedroom, singing a cheerful tune.

He changed into jeans and a blue plaid flannel shirt. Not wanting to work tonight, but obligated to do so, he ground his teeth together and laced his pair of work boots. After tonight he'd have enough to pay off Patty. Free of liability, his mind focused on the prize. Tomorrow he planned to ask Shania to marry him in front of his loved ones. Tom Moran, his fraternity brother and best man, came to Cyan for the weekend to share in his happiness. Morgan had invited Shania's parents, hoping to bridge the gap now that time had healed the wounds. One more night and Shania would be officially engaged to him.

Excitement made his pulse rate increase as he reentered the family room to find her getting a sketch book from her portfolio. Justin waited by the French doors holding a red ball in his gloved hands. Sighting Morgan, he bounced up and down making his sneakers light. A few slices of bread lay on top of a paper towel on the brown, cream and black speckled counter top. He grabbed the bread, then unlocked the door.

"You have an hour until dinner's ready," Shania said.

Morgan glanced at the table set for three. One chair had a stack of thick business office catalogs and books on the seat. He'd need to get a booster seat for Justin. "Okay, honey."

"Okay, honey," Justin piped.

Morgan threw open the door and the energetic kid ran into the yard. The squawking and barking of the geese scared Justin at first. Morgan showed him how to tear off a piece of the square bread and toss it as hard as he could to the center for the flock. Feathers flew, beaks clashed and the harsh cries continued. A few more morsels sailed through the air and a scurry of pecking commenced. The feathered creatures made enough racket guzzling down the carbs, they could awaken the spirits living near the water.

"Do you want to try the last piece?"

Justin's glance traveled from Morgan to the bread and then to the gaggle of geese. Justin tilted his blond topped head and narrowed his blue-green eyes. He didn't resemble his mother in appearance, although in personality he was indeed her son. He blew out a breath and tightened his jaw as he lowered the ball to the ground. His gaze remained on the flock as he removed one glove. Morgan handed him a chunk of whole wheat bread. Justin took the slice and tore off a piece. He hurled it like a shot-put toward the sand. A goose ran forward, caught the bread mid-air, and choked the large portion. He just barely avoided other members from taking the treasure by scuttling backward.

"Whoa!" Justin's eyes widened, as bright as silver dollars.

"He's a determined bird." Morgan chuckled. "Finish it off. We'll kick around the ball for a while."

Justin tore the slice of bread into three sections and tossed the handful of crumbs into the gaggle. Feathers flew. The squawking created a symphony of quacks and honks.

Morgan glanced at the house. Shania stood at the windows, her fingers moved a pencil in quick sharp motions across a sketch pad.

"Okay." Justin wiped his fingers on his jeans, put the glove on, and picked up the orb.

They kicked the ball around and tossed the now cold rubber in a game of catch. Morgan glanced at his watch. He had half an hour left to eat and get as many kisses from Shania as possible.

As Justin ran past to fetch the ball, Morgan grabbed him and tickled the exposed tender skin between his coat and pants. "Come on, we need to go eat dinner."

The wiggling stopped. Morgan set him on his feet.

"Okay." Justin pulled his coat down and picked up the ball. "I love you, Daddy."

Morgan's pulse rate ramped as fast as the flapping of the bird's wings. His throat closed off. His child rammed a fiery blade into his heart. His life was rich and full having Shania and Justin as part of his world. He couldn't have wished for more. He didn't try to hide the tears forming in his eyes. "I love you too, son."

He scooped Justin into his arms and headed toward the house. "Let's eat, I'm hungry."

"Me too. We get ice cream for dessert." Justin licked his lips.

"I like ice cream." Morgan smiled, enjoying the simple pleasures of life.

Morgan opened the door and shut it with his foot. He placed Justin on the counter top beside the sink, removed his gloves and coat, and turned on the warm water. "Wash your hands."

Justin stuck his fingers under the liquid and Morgan squirted soap onto a small palm. A quick wash and he handed Justin a towel. Morgan lowered him onto his makeshift seat and glanced around for Shania. The hallway bath door opened. A moment later she stood beside her chair. He pulled out the seat.

She gracefully sat, then Morgan lowered beside her on the sturdy wood.

"Did you get a lot of studying done?"

She shrugged and placed food on Justin's plate. She cut the pieces into bite-sized portions. "I've a lot on my mind and can't seem to focus."

"I'll help you study later." He took a plate and placed a few scoops of mouth-watering vegetables and beef on it. Morgan set the dish in front of her. Next he loaded his stoneware.

"Sounds great." She set Justin's plate in front of him.

"I'd like to say grace before we start." Morgan slipped his napkin on his lap.

She grabbed the plate from Justin. "Baby doll, we're going to say a prayer to thank God for providing us with this food."

Justin looked at her, at the plate and then at Morgan. Obviously prayer wasn't a ritual for them. She came from a strict, religious family. Was part of her rebellion rejecting the practice of her parents?

"Thank you, Lord, for this meal and for my loved ones being safe and by my side. Amen." He kept his gaze on Justin, who held his hands in prayer mode. Shania's hands were hidden under the table.

"Amen," Justin declared a moment later, and Shania placed the food in front of him.

"What job are you going to after dinner, Morgan?" she asked as she took her fork into hand.

"It's a construction site on Toad Lane. A few more days and I'll be finished. It'll be nice to go back to ten hour days." He tasted the roast, cooked to perfection.

"Can I have ice cream now?" Justin asked.

"You'll need to eat some of your vegetables first," Shania responded, buttered a slice of sweet yeast-scented bread and placed it on the smaller plate.

"This is excellent, Shania. Your cooking skills have certainly improved." He grinned, referring to the gumbo she'd made one Sunday a couple of years ago, the last time she'd prepared a meal for him. From the glint in her eyes she understood.

"Hey, I followed the directions, it wasn't my fault they were incorrect. I don't understand how a recipe for beginner cooks wouldn't be verified." She laughed. "The soup did have a stinky foot smell, didn't it?"

"That's saying it nicely." The ping of a fork hitting the tile floor added tempo to his words.

"But we found a new bistro that served excellent tomato-basil, and I've had time to hone my craft." She handed a new fork to Justin.

"I don't like the green things," Justin declared.

"Well, you did a great job with the carrots and the potatoes have certainly been plowed, so I can't determine how much of them you've eaten." She lifted his bread, one set of teeth marks were visible. "What do you think, Morgan?"

Justin looked at him, hope in his eyes.

"I think he should have some ice cream."

"Yeah." Justin kicked his chair. Green lights sparkled from his shoes.

Shania stood, walked to the refrigerator and extracted organic ice cream. Vanilla. Morgan's favorite.

"Cherries?" Justin asked and twisted in his chair to look at her.

"Morgan, do you have cherries?" She scooped a small amount of ice cream into a plastic coffee cup with a John Deere tractor decal on the outside, compliments of Murray Tractor Supply.

"Maybe. Check the cupboard to the left of the refrigerator." He glanced at his watch. Fifteen minutes.

The door squeaked open. "Oh," she softly said.

"Cherries?" Justin exuberant voice kept tempo with his heels cracking against the wood.

Morgan glanced at Shania. Damn, he should have looked for the fruit himself.

She held out a bag of orange peanut-shaped candies. "You hate circus peanuts."

Heat rose to his face as she looked at the tag.

"You kept them, from when we went to the circus three years ago? They're not going to be good. Why, if you don't like them, did you keep them?" She held the bag in her palm and studied his face.

"Because…" He placed his napkin on the table and went to her. "I have to leave for work. See you around ten."

He kissed her; a warm, lusty, joining of lips he hoped would leave her dazed. Anything to take her attention away from his secret mementos of their fun times together. Grabbing the cup of ice cream, he set it in front of Justin. He kissed his son's forehead and hurried out of the house before she could further witness his embarrassment.

Chapter 14

Morgan stepped into the guest room directly across from the master suite. The pull-out bed had been lined with pillows to prevent Justin from rolling off the sides. His shoes were neatly lined up under the bed--sneakers and then the taller red cowboy boots. He snuggled the blue blanket Morgan had given him as an infant close to his chin. The material becoming ragged at the edges after three years of frequent washings. Quiet breaths of air came from his open mouth.

A soft glow came from the master bedroom. Morgan moved toward it, pressing the door open. Her beauty created a thump inside his chest. His lungs filled to the point they did not fit into the allotted space. Shania had the ability to do that to him--literally stop his breath.

She held a book as thin as a dime in front of her. Her tea-colored eyes narrowed as she focused on the text. A scowl formed on her make-up free face. He closed the door and walked over to his dresser.

"Hi, what's wrong?" He exhaled. Removing his wallet, he placed it on the dresser top. His fingers unlatched his belt and dropped it to the floor.

"Hi back, how'd the second job go?" She tapped the book against her hand.

"I'm glad I'm done. All night I couldn't wait to see you and Justin. How's studying going?"

She shook her head and ran her fingers through the short crop of hairs. "I can't comprehend all of this marketing crap."

"Let me wash off some of this dust, and I'll take a look." He winked. "Maybe I can help with the confusion." He gathered clothing from the antique maple dresser.

"Oh, right, you majored in business and marketing. Sorry about the bad attitude, I'm stressed." She shoved the covers down, revealing her slim legs and sensual-perfect feet. No hammer toes on his woman.

"You need help in the shower?" She raised an eyebrow. Why was it a simple forehead wrinkle tempted him more than her husky, arousing telephone voice? He glanced to her pixie hair, ruffled from dragging her fingers through the locks. For some odd reason her dishevelment captivated him.

He sucked in his breath.

"Hell, yes, but I know you need to study." He smiled at her. "Could I take a rain-check for the assistance in the shower?"

His cock threatened to pop over the top of his underwear. She'd dressed in a tank top and another pair of those barely-there panties. Uplifted pointed nipples drew his attention. She coughed, bringing his notice to her bottom lip, red from the pressure of her teeth. He refocused on her eyes sparkling with happiness and desire. She'd had a rough three years. The pleasure of being with her, seeing her carefree, and bantering about having sex with him made his dick ready to split open like a sausage on a hot grill.

Four long years, he'd loved her. He was close to having her become a permanent part of his life. Morgan wanted to dance around the room.

"Sure," she agreed. She winked at him and smoothed her curls. He decided right then that he liked her short sexy hair.

Morgan alternated between a cold and hot shower. He didn't want to kill the hard-on. The lesson he had in mind for helping her understand marketing required concentration, not a distraction from his vibrating cock. He dried off and wrapped a towel around his hips. Later he'd put on boxers in case Justin came in, which was unlikely because the kid was a deep sleeper. Morgan wanted to be free and accessible. Despite the chill from the frigid water infusion, he was hanging high underneath the cotton as he walked into the bedroom.

He shoved the covers to the side, plumped the pillows at his back and rested beside Shania. He moved his legs, brushing against hers. "What are we working with here?"

Morgan smiled as she shifted her gaze away from his half-naked form and handed him the slender book. "We're studying lateral marketing based on Philip Kotler's process—"

"This isn't Kotler's book." He waved the thin journal.

"I know. Kotler's book is on the dining room chair. Justin was using it as a booster seat." Lifting she tucked her legs to sit cross-legged and faced him. Her gaze went south.

"Difficult to study the father of lateral marketing if his words are being used as a riser." He grinned. She frowned. He stopped his laughter from erupting.

"Yes, well, I think it's the perfect place for him. Anyway, I understood his social marketing concepts, so I'm able to grasp the idea of products and competitors. The lateral thing is baffling me." Some strands of hair stood on end as she finger-combed her locks. She sighed and dropped her arm between them. His hand ached to smooth down the ruffled curls.

He grabbed the pieces of paper from the nightstand and glanced over her faultless handwriting. "Reviewing your notes, the hub of lateral marketing is creative technique. The marketer wants to solidify a connection, or make a displacement." He rubbed her palm, light minute circles through the middle down to her wrist and over the mound under her thumb as he glanced through the pages. "Let's do direct application."

"Meaning?"

"Okay, what you're really referring to is a gap or detachment from the product on the current market and the concept." He held up her hand, continuing to caress her palm.

"First you'll want to substitute it, replace the focus." He moved his thumb from her palm and replaced the digit with his lips.

"I understand that concept very well." She hummed.

"Change it to be opposite. Currently you are facing me cross-legged. If you were to move, lie down ..."

She lay back on the bed, arms loosely joined on her stomach.

He placed her arms snug against her sides and separated her clasped knees. "Opposite."

"Combine the stimulus." He moved one of her arms to rest on his shoulder and kissed her slightly open lips. He caressed her taut nipples, rubbed his toes against the inside of her foot, and then broke the connection. "Ah, a sensitive area."

"Umm, by far my favorite part of displacement," she murmured.

"Exaggerate the marketing tool by maxing the product out or taking most of it away." He drew away, leaving only his finger stroking the side of her breast. Another shower would be in order if he continued along this path. His skin was moist, his cock as hard as a steel hammer.

"I believe adding more of the product, your mouth, will work better for me." She licked her lips. Her eyes blazed with heat and lust. Fingers reached and caressed his skin, creating havoc. Hot desire flooded him.

"The last two concepts are eliminating the product. Think about what the item would look like if the focus wasn't on it." He let his finger slide off her body. "You want the consumer to center his or her attention on the merchandise."

"No," she breathed and turned her body, connecting her hips to his.

"Then the final concept would be to reorder." He kissed her lips, consuming her mouth.

She placed her hand at the side of his face and rolled her pelvis against his stiff cock. "I'd like to reorder, please."

He smiled, praying patience would remain solid. "Changing an aspect of the product, need, target or occasion, according to Kotler, is the easiest way to go about lateral marketing." He outlined her lips with his tongue. "Change the need--re-target the product to satisfy another need."

"Throw out some ideas. I'm on board." She ripped off his towel, exposing his product.

He took small deep breaths. He didn't want to rush the moment. How could he resist when the air between them heated to the point of inferno level?

"First, start with the bare…ah…item for consumption." He slid his fingers under her tank and painstakingly drew the material past her breasts, holding it at her neck.

"This little touch of silk must go. If you lift, I'll slide the material off your body instead of ripping it off with my teeth, which my mind is urging me to do." He breathed through his nose and out his mouth, as if he were running a marathon again.

"Let me see, lose the garment but have your mouth on my body or save the cloth and no mouth?" She nibbled on his nipple. "You tell me, love, do you like my lips on your body?"

"Yes. Mouth." He was losing the power. The mentor was becoming the student, and he adored being under her lips' tutelage. Off came the tank top. She could be the aggressor tonight, create a new method of give and take. Their relationship had indeed grown from a friendship to love.

"I do understand quid pro quo." She shoved his shoulder.

He rested against the propped pillow, watching her give homage to his body, reversing the lesson he'd taught her. Her artistic fingers stroked his chest, caressed his stomach, and gently kneaded his dick. He lifted his hips when she massaged his balls. Not wishing to rush, needing to slow down his breathing, he used Lamaze breathing. His fingers clutched the sheets underneath him as her mouth latched onto his penis. Her tongue swirled and wrapped around his head. Her teeth nipped the sensitive point.

Oh, shit, this was torture. His breathing became ragged. He closed his eyes and focused on mundane matters, trying to prevent an explosion.

The rattle of foil being peeled brought his attention back. She was rolling a condom on his pulsating cock. She straddled his hips. Her lips attacked his, as he guided his penis into the slick warmth of her vagina.

She was hot, tight and gyrated with precision. Her hands braced each side of his head. Eyes closed, she leaned back. Her breasts bobbled as she lifted and lowered, rubbing her nubile body against his. His hands massaged her breasts, rolled her nipples. The heat and sweat so intense he hesitated. She wavered. Fearing she'd lose her time, tempo, he moved his hands to her waist and guided her, creating a sync.

They found a rhythm of love and lust. Fulfillment rushed into a blending of them becoming one, until she collapsed onto his chest.

She kissed his sweaty chest. "I think I'm going to enjoy our study sessions."

"Yes, we should study every night." His lips touched her forehead.

"How are you with creative dance?"

Chapter 15

Shania stood on an eight-foot stepladder in his living room, a white towel sprinkled with fuzzy bits of gray gripped in her hands. Justin moved toys around in a play area in the middle of the floor, making noises to fit the vehicle.

"Shania, what are you doing?" Morgan cringed as his voice came out louder than he'd intended.

She jerked and the stepladder shifted. "Dusting."

He ran forward. "Get down," he demanded.

She glanced at the clock, a couple of inches away from where she stood and swiped a piece of cloth over the edge of the shelf. "What are you doing home so early?"

"I couldn't concentrate. Thoughts of you clouded my mind." She'd entered his life in a new and better way. He wanted to capitalize on his luck of having her and Justin in his home. He shifted projects and left. The first time in five years of owning his business he allowed others to take control of ventures. He delayed jobs, and it was a result of the woman teetering on a ladder in his living room.

Shania stared at him. Her tiger eyes glittered with curiosity. "Why?"

She stood at the top, on the *Do not stand on this step* portion of an eight-foot ladder. A grimy cloth grasped in her hand rested on a shelf another foot above her head.

His panic of her falling ramped his blood pressure pumping to high-speed. He neared the edge of the ladder. "Shania, get down, please."

She took a step lower and narrowed her eyes. "I didn't want to study, and I noticed a cobweb."

"Mommy's going to time out," Justin chortled from the middle of the colorful play area. Morgan's favorite Cubs blanket had been used to create a tent in the corner of the room.

The kid knew how to read his mother's facial expressions. She grimaced, pivoted, and lost her footing. Morgan's heart, near to stopping, didn't fail him as he caught her. His arms wrapped around her and lowered her to the floor, safely away from the fireplace ledge. She twisted around, bringing them face-to-face and placed her hands on top of his at her sides.

She gazed into his eyes. "The last time you caught me falling from a ladder we were painting the little house on Beeker Street. Remember?" Her tiny white teeth clasped onto her lower lip.

"You used that horrible baby-poop yellow color of paint." The memory warmed him. He kissed her cheek, thankful he finally caught her—forever. She moved her arms to rest on his shoulders, her palms rubbing back and forth, the gesture connecting them as lovers. His hands stroked her back.

She chuckled and nodded. "The paint was more baby-poop than mustard. No diggidy, no doubt."

She must have found the fresh bag of candies in the cupboard with the circus peanuts, as a spicy scent wafted in the air. He loved those tiny cinnamon dots she always ate.

He laughed. "Diggidy, right. Dr. Dre was your musician of choice during that week."

"Yep. The paint hit the wall, and I figured out why the can was in the discount bin at Hank's Hardware." She inhaled. "I love your spicy cologne."

She leaned into him close enough that the contact with his chest hardened her nipples. He wanted to lay her down on the sofa, strip the winter garments off, and rub his hands up and down her bare skin. He exhaled. This wasn't the time or place. Justin played nearby. Morgan lowered his arms and inhaled, taking in her scent.

"The walls looked nice enough after you put that stain on top," Morgan murmured.

"It was a faux treatment, meant to make the walls look like aged stone." She finger-combed his hair. He put his face next to hers, stroking her soft skin with his cheek. His stomach tightened in anticipation of a kiss.

"Considering you wouldn't let me patch the walls, the room certainly had that cracked ruins ambiance." He wove his fingers with hers tugging her, around the toys and Justin, to the sofa.

"Don't you have to go to work?" Hands clasped, she stepped over a monster truck, reached the couch and plopped onto the firm cushion. He sat beside her.

"Nope, I've the day free to spend with you and Justin." He rubbed the inside of her palm with the pad of his thumb, replaying their lovemaking from last night.

"Feed the ducks?" Justin hinted. He parked his miniature pick-up truck near the other antique toys. His rrrr sputtering motor sounds created music in the room.

Morgan had dragged the toy box from his parents' attic. He'd played with the metal trucks, cars, and farm equipment replicas as a youngster and not one of them converted into a robot. The collectibles certainly weren't old enough to be considered antiques. If they were, he was one as well. He touched the crinkles at the edges of his eyes. Did Shania think of him as old?

* * * *

Shania gazed into Morgan's face, trying to determine why he'd come home early. A workaholic, he wouldn't just drop everything because he was thinking of her. Stomach fluttering, heart pounding at a quicker rate, she hoped he might have done just that.

He smiled and nodded to Justin. "Since it's almost lunchtime, I thought we'd get carry-out and have a picnic in the shelter at Witch Hazel's Park. Then, if it's okay with your mom, we'll go to my parents' ranch and play with the horses." Morgan moved his glance from Justin to her. His green eyes held a questioning glint.

Had their shift in relationship from friends to lovers changed the playing field? He'd waited nearly three months to track her down at Briarwood. And what about Justin? Morgan had been his surrogate father since birth. The new dynamics would affect each of them. It would be impossible to go back to being simply friends.

"Horses," Justin screamed. Toy truck in hand, he ran straight into Morgan's spread legs and crashed into the sensitive V between his thighs. Morgan's hands shot over to protect his privates, but wheels and bumper connected. Shania shoved her hand to her mouth in an attempt to stifle the laughter begging for release.

"Yes, horses." Morgan grimaced and dropped the truck to the floor. He lifted Justin to sit beside him.

"I think it sounds like an excellent idea. Justin, you need to put your toys away," Shania said.

Justin scooted off the sofa and picked up the monster truck. Carefully carrying the toy to the box, he placed it in the bottom. His thick jeans would keep him warm, but she'd need to add a sweater over the flannel shirt. She hadn't had a chance to shop for a winter coat. Although the air was chilly, his lightweight jacket would suffice.

"Do you have time? I know you wanted to study," he whispered into her ear, stirring the fine hairs, multiplying the tingle in her stomach and ache between her thighs.

"Yes, plenty of time." Her head turned a fraction of an inch. He placed his work-worn callused hand on the side of her cheek, close to her mouth. Physically she had to touch him and kissed his palm.

She eliminated the space, breathed in his spearmint-scented breath. She shut her eyes, wanting to taste his lips, wanting his touch to be in her memory, wanting to recognize his kiss without a visual.

"Ready?" Justin asked.

Shania opened her eyes and glanced at Justin, boasting a wide smile and coat in hand.

Morgan groaned. "Yes, just a second." He sucked in his breath, dropped his hand to his knee, digging into the denim, and shifted on the sofa.

Shania shot Morgan a half smile and scooted to the edge of the seat. "Come on, Justin, I think it'd be a good idea to use the bathroom and wash your hands before we go."

"Come on, Daddy, you too." Justin tugged Morgan's hand.

"Okay." He sat forward.

Shania rose from the settee and snagged Morgan's free hand. "Come on."

"No fair, two against one." Morgan pulled both of them into his arms and in turn nuzzled each of their necks.

Justin giggled.

"More," Shania cooed.

"More for you later." Morgan snickered. She kissed his cheek and wiggled out of his one-armed embrace.

"I'll get a sweatshirt for Justin. Do you need one?" She winked at him. His skin begged to be touched. Morgan wore a moss green long-sleeved polo. A white cotton t-shirt underneath showed between the V.

"I'll be fine with my jacket. The temperature is a balmy forty degrees today. We didn't get the expected snow, but it'll come before Christmas." He stood and tucked Justin under his arm, carrying him like a football. "Good idea to get the kid a sweatshirt though. We don't want snotty noses in our house."

Our house. Her stomach flipped like a fish on dry land.

"I don't have a snotty nose," Justin bellowed.

* * * *

Shania smiled as Justin raced ahead of her, his path leading straight to the corral. He bypassed a Merle, black-tan-white, collie prancing beside the fence. On a different day he would've taken the time to pet the dog. However, every five minutes from the time he found out about the horses, he'd asked when they'd get to see them. They scrapped the park visit and after a quick meal at La Casa's, they went to the Hardwicks' ranch. Justin climbed the log hewn fence to perch beside Morgan.

She glanced at him. Morgan planted one work boot on a lower rail, acting as a barrier in case Justin flew backward from his perch on the top rail. Justin hugged the wood beam. His head swiveled back and forth watching brown, beige and mixed quarter horses huddled in groups at the corners. A single stately black stud trotted along the fence in a pen by himself, his tail lifted high in the air.

"Can I ride one?" Justin asked.

"Not alone," Morgan replied.

Shania shot a wide-eyed glance to Morgan and quietly stated, "Not at all. He's only three."

"I'll take him for a short ride, Morgan," a deep male voice stated.

Shania pivoted to see Morgan's father striding forward. She released the breath caught in her throat, forcing the fear outside. "I don't—"

"If that's all right with you, Shania? Maybe you and Morgan would like to take a ride. I'll take the little guy for a nice easy canter." He winked at Justin, who stared at him and the black-thick coated horse beside him, standing at least fifteen hands high. The man and the stallion held her son's interest. "Then, we'll get a piece of the best chocolate cake this side of the Missouri."

"Mr. Hardwick—"

"Now, Shania, I told you years ago to call me Mark." He smiled, Morgan's sweet cocky smile replicated in the older man. Both had dark blond hair, although Mark's contained a liberal sprinkling of gray. Carolina blue eyes were surrounded by age-defining wrinkles. At six feet, he was two inches shorter than Morgan. His heart--equal in size.

"Dad, Justin's a little small to be prancing around on Black Knight." Morgan lowered Justin to the ground and grabbed her hand from fluttering in the air, as she attempted to snag Justin's coat. He held her fingers tight.

"I'm a big boy," Justin blustered.

"You were riding solo at three, but it's different when your son wants to ride a horse as big as an eight-wheeler's cab." Mark's hooded eyes didn't give away his thoughts.

Shania jerked at the statement and glanced at Morgan. His stare didn't hold remorse, only a happy glow. She shouldn't have been surprised Morgan told his parents about Justin.

"I haven't seen this little guy since he was a baby. It'd be nice to talk with him." Mark held out his hand. "Hi, Justin. Remember me? I'm Mark, Morgan's dad."

Justin's fingers dug into the wood rail. He faced Morgan's father and then glanced at Morgan, who responded with a cockeyed grin. Justin held out his free right hand. "I'll do it. Bob the Builder rode a horse. I can too."

Mark took Justin's hand in his. "Morgan, if you and Shania plan to ride, you might want to start. The sky's clouding. Rain will be coming soon."

Shania glanced at Mark, at the horses and then the pout on her son's face. Justin read her decision and whooped.

Justin jumped from the rail. He and Mark walked toward the barn. "Who's Bob the Builder?"

Justin described a cartoon whose occupation was making things. He compared Bob to his daddy.

Morgan pulled her to his side. "Do you want to take a ride…together?"

Butterflies tickled her stomach at the thought of riding in front of Morgan on the back of a fine stallion. Her mind kept slipping back to Justin riding a horse, the black one that stood as tall as her Jeep. As a mother, she needed to loosen the strings, but couldn't. As a veterinarian, Mark understood the ins and outs of animals. Nothing would happen to Justin. Right? Parenting was becoming more difficult. Shania anticipated at the onset of Justin talking that it would be smooth sailing thereon out because he could tell her what he needed, wanted, or where he hurt. No. Not true. Verbal skills created independence for him and new critical decision making on her end. This happened to be one of those times.

"He'll be fine. My father knows his way around horses." Morgan tilted his Stetson. He kissed her cheek. "I know of a place in the woods. Abandoned. Sad, but true. Stone exterior, created in the early nineteenth century. Are you interested in taking a look at the house? For creative art purposes of course."

"You do know how to distract a girl." She leaned her head against his chest and watched Mark ride out on a pretty dark brown mare. Justin clutched the saddle horn, his face tight with a mix of fear and excitement. Mark leaned down and said something to him. Justin smiled. As they rode past he clung to the horn. He was as stubborn as she and would subdue the fright to have the experience.

Shania twitched.

Morgan held her hand firmly in his. "He'll be fine. The first couple of bumps are always scary."

She glanced from the rear of the horse to Morgan. "You're right, but he's still a baby…my baby."

"You'll need to let him explore life. Come on. I haven't been on my stallion in months. I'd like to take him out for a ride. Are you game?" He tugged the hat firmly on his head and pulled her toward the barn.

"What's his name?" She glanced at the brown mare and listened for any signs of distress from Justin. Exuberant laughter resonated in the wind. Her son would be fine.

"Silver Star," he said.

They walked into the barn. A flashback of her first visit to Morgan's parents came to mind. Her parents had shunned her, Beck's parents denied her, but Mark and Maggie welcomed her with open arms. She'd mooned around the first couple of days, and then Mark put her to work. Before the sun opened the day, they'd ousted her from under the warm green, blue and white wedding ring quilt.

She'd dressed in sweatpants, riding boots and one of Morgan's discarded flannel shirts. A quick cup of hot chocolate and a slice of toast later, she'd trailed Mark to the barn. He guided her through his method of grooming the massive draft horses. She'd never forget how much pleasure the simple act of brushing the rough hairs of a stud or filly's coat gave her. She garnered a sense of accomplishment and peace invigorated her as the beasts moaned with each stroke. Her stress lessened as it did now, standing in the exact spot nearly four years later.

Morgan led her into the stables and the pleasurable aroma of hay wafted into her nostrils—not excluding the pungent odor of feces. She ran her fingers over the embossed name, Windfall. The steed's legs moved forward, stirring the straw dust underneath. She touched his velvety soft snout.

"I feel at home here. For some reason when I'm around your parents, and even just by walking into this building, I get a sense of comfort. I'm not sure how to describe it. Security, maybe?" She scratched behind the horse's white ears. Windfall blew out a rush of air and shook his head, his gray nose standing out against the pearl of the rest of his body.

"I understand. I feel the same way. I've given some thought to how relaxed I become when I visit here. Simplify. I believe people should make their lives simpler. By not expecting so much and living an uncomplicated life they will be happier. My parents, conservationists before it became the norm, only invest in necessary products and try not to pollute the air." He sat down on a bale of hay. "And at dinner, they say grace to thank God for the gifts granted them. Simplicity." His soft words flowed over her like warm water, relaxing her muscles. The angst of her son riding on a giant horse lessened.

"Simplicity." She kneed Morgan's legs apart and rested her wrists on his broad shoulders. "I'm all for reducing stress and appreciating the gifts given to me."

Shania tilted his hat and smoothed her fingers across his forehead and cheek. "I'm especially thankful you tracked me down in Briarwood."

His arms wrapped around her waist. "Why didn't you leave me your forwarding address, or tell me of your plans to move to Briarwood?"

His voice, even in tone, held a hint of reproach.

"Morgan, I tried--"

"Morgan, here's Silver Star. He's anxious to get on a good run. Are you sure you don't want me to saddle another horse for Ms. Miller?" George, the caretaker, asked. Mark must have requested the stallion to be prepared.

Morgan dropped his hands. Shania experienced cold regret and sudden fear. She stepped away and glanced at George. He'd been a member of the Hardwick family since the age of ten. He'd been given a job as a stable boy and he never left. Now he was stoop-shouldered, gray-haired, and his long nose appeared to have continued to grow, as did his smile. "Hi, George. Do you think Mollie misses me?"

"Cantankerous old goat. She needs to be put out to pasture. Draft horses take up space and eat buckets of food." George rubbed his gnarled hand over Silver Star's neck.

Shania chuckled. "I take that as a 'yes, she misses me.'"

George tugged a small apple out of his jacket pocket and handed it to her. "See for yourself."

She took the apple and glanced at Morgan. "I'll be right back."

Two mares down, Mollie nibbled on the side of the stall. "Hey, Mollie!" Shania handed the large work horse the apple, then gave her a quick hug. Mollie pawed the ground as she bit into the fresh aromatic fruit. Shania hurried to the entrance. Morgan led Silver Star out of the barn and into the yard.

The aroma of leather and horse added to the crisp late fall air. Morgan slipped his hands around her waist and hoisted her onto the saddle. He slid behind her, hips touching. She tingled from the contact. His fingers grazed her thigh as he gripped the straps, then guided the steed down the lane to the meadow. She used the horn to reposition, resting her body snug against Morgan's.

"Back to your question. You were marrying Patty, and if I couldn't …" She twisted to look into his face. "I thought you'd married her. You deserved the freedom to start your life together."

"I couldn't stay with you the night of the wedding. I had obligations to Patty and to my family." His strong arm tugged her to connect with his chest. "The next day you were gone. No note. No forwarding address, nothing."

The gentle sway of the mount across the hard ground relaxed her, allowing her to contemplate his response. "I needed to leave. Start over. I didn't even know if you'd gone ahead and married her."

"We both made mistakes, but today we have a fresh start—together. Look, there's an elderberry bush. Can you believe the berries are still clinging to the vine?" His breath warmed her ear.

She glanced at the black seeds. "Yes," she croaked out, lust-fire burning a hole in her stomach.

"If you sleep under an elderberry bush on a midsummer night, you'll dream of the man you're to marry. Do you think you'd dream of me?"

"Yes." Marry! Thump clomp, thump clomp. Her heart flapped against her chest as hard as the equine's steel hooves hit the ground. Glad she hadn't worn the cap, she turned her head. If she leaned a fraction of an inch his lips would brush her face. "Why did you take so long to contact me?"

"I had a situation to resolve before I could find out if we had a future. And I doubted myself." He gave her a brief stroke on her cheek at the edge of her mouth, his hand tightened on her waist.

"Do you plan to have a future with us?" she questioned as her stomach heaved in rebellion. What if he said "maybe" or "no"?

"You better believe it," he trumpeted.

She relaxed as he continued to describe the winter berry bushes and various types of trees. He didn't ask any questions, which was good because she couldn't reply with clear logical contemplation or repeat what he had stated. Her thoughts focused on him, their future, and what his touch did to her senses.

His fingers rested against her coat, not in contact with her skin but she could feel the burn. Her pulse rode along her veins at a quicker pace.

His spearmint-scented breath tickled the side of her face. Her cheek gravitated toward his perfect lips. As she hoped, he kissed her. Simple sweet connections, making her feel more in love with him. They were blending together like oils on a canvas, no harsh lines, just simple pure beauty.

"Up here on the right is the structure. I say structure because only the shell remains. Unfortunately, it's late afternoon and overcast. There won't be sun shining down and highlighting the best features." As Morgan made the statement, the glimmer of sun peeking behind a cloud lost its luster. The sky blanketed with clouds, creating an ominous gloom.

"What was the building used for?" The answer was obvious, but she wanted his lips close to her face again.

"Originally, as a family home, then a caretaker's place, and today, an inspirational site for my fiancée." He tucked his cheek against hers as the house came into view.

Fiancée. She lifted upward easing the tingling. His knees squeezed her thighs. Desire rocketed through her, heating her. She wanted to be his bride and practice marketing every night.

"The ramshackle house's solid foundation remains firm despite the roof having caved in recently. Last time I was here the porch collapsed to the point of joining roof to floor. Obviously, it should be taken down." He stopped the horse within feet of the overgrown hedge or vines or weeds of some sort.

She loved the exterior. Washed gray stone had battled the test of time. Broken paned windows provided a peek into the interior. A small preacher's cap at the top of the second story remained intact. Vines had woven in the remaining black and rusted steel of the casement. The rotten door hung askew. The cottage style rounded wood had, at one time, created a soft romantic entry. "I'd like to see the inside if possible."

Morgan hadn't responded. She glanced at him. Even with his Stetson shading his face, his eyes were narrowed as if evaluating the situation.

"We'll peek inside. If the interior appears dangerous, I'll do whatever you wish, back out, go forward. You'll be calling the shots," she offered. From his silence and intense evaluation of the house she anticipated "no" as the answer.

He stared.

She blinked.

The corners of his mouth lifted.

She grinned. His actions were so similar to Justin's she wanted to weep with happiness.

"I go first." His smile widened. Green eyes glittered.

Shania nodded, holding the victory laughter inside. She slipped her right leg over the saddle horn, and slid to the ground. Silver Star shied a step.

Morgan patted the steed's neck and spoke softly into his ear. "Whoa, there, there."

Silver Star snorted, stopped his sidestep. A moment later he settled.

Morgan dismounted, then flung the leads over the saddle. Shania admired the faith he had in his mount not to take flight, a true telling of the measure of the man. Loyalty and trust were a part of Morgan's character as shown by his horse, family and friends.

Due to the late November frost, a path had formed from decaying weeds. Morgan tucked her hand into his and led the way to the steps. He gingerly stepped onto the wooden portico, keeping her at arm's length. The scent of decayed wood and aromatic plant life created a private conservatory. She loved the ambience, old world but strong and reliable because of the solid foundation—just like Morgan.

"Take small steps, follow my trail." He dropped her hand.

His footprints were obvious in the dirt covered porch. She stepped in his shoe imprints, making their path become one. Her breath faltered. She'd always follow him, anywhere on Earth as long as they could be together. The squeak of metal against metal brought her attention to Morgan. He shoved the door open. She held steady as he glanced inside.

"There is a barrel size hole in the floor about two feet in front of the opening. We'll avoid the crater and keep to the right side."

"Right. Got it," she replied.

He stepped farther into the house. She passed over the threshold. He slid his arm around her waist drawing her close to his side. Rotten boards had fallen inward or upward as a large tree branch had plummeted through the roof. In the middle of the room, a dead, leafless, potted plant's thick end leaned against the fireplace, blocking the opening. The natural stone hearth covered a good portion of the wall. Muted light continued to filter through. A moment of sun created illuminating shadows on the partitions and floor.

Branches had decayed and fallen into the floor's hole, plugging the cracks. The musty scent of the flora added to the romance of the house. A staircase to the left had a broken banister. The ragged moth-eaten oriental rug at one time had padded the steps.

"It's beautiful," she whispered. She turned into his arms, gazed at him. The cloudy day seemed brighter as a result of being alone with Morgan, by having him in her life.

"Not as beautiful as you," he replied. Her chest expanded as she absorbed his sincerity.

His lips pressed against her cheek. "I think any structure built on a solid foundation will stand the test of time and survive any damages that may come along."

By the glint in his eyes, he referred to their relationship as well as the cottage. If she hadn't already been in love with him, that moment would have convinced her that Morgan Hardwick was the one for her. His consideration was undeniable. His heroic caring attitude made her admiration for him expand with pride and adoration.

As he wrapped both arms snug around her, he kissed her. "Shania, I want to ask you to…"

Thunder rumbled. Sharp swords of white slashed into the now dark space. Silver Star whined.

She inhaled the scent of the impending downpour and placed her gloved hand on Morgan's broad chest. "Yes, Morgan."

Another reverberating rumble followed by a strike of lighting illuminated their intimate space. A dash of wind blew broken twigs and leaves into tiny cyclones.

"Damn, I didn't plan this very well. I want to talk to you, but not rush the words out like a gusher. We should leave. The cold November rain will chill us to the bones if we get caught in the torrent." Hands clasped, he shoved aside a broken branch, and led her out of their secret place.

Had he wanted to tell her he loved her? To ask her to marry him--for real?

Chapter 16

Shania put the finishing touches on the painting of Morgan and Justin feeding the ducks she'd sketched a few days before. She had created two pieces as gifts for Morgan's mother and father. One etching defined Morgan's exquisite side view. The plain, pencil-sketched portrait exhibited his wonderful character, the glint in his eye and the lifted corner of his mouth.

The duck scene deserved color. She had limited materials to work with, a sketch pad made of high-end cotton, and artist-quality oil pastel crayons. A blending of the oils challenged her. She started with the brown grasses in the corner of the page getting a feel for the smudging and merging. The grease paints flowed, filling in the background. Their faces were a trifle more difficult. She found a couple of cotton tips and toothpicks to help her form the details. Quite pleased with the final result, she celebrated by dancing around the room. Morgan's midnight blue jacket and Justin's crimson coat made the picture pop with vibrancy.

Morgan had created two plain mission-style frames before he left to fix a tenant's plumbing problem. She ran her fingers over the smooth wood, appreciating his exceptional carpentry.

She glanced at the kitchen clock, two hours until dinner. He would arrive soon. They would drive her car, to his parents' house, since it had the child seat strapped in, and could fit a family better than the truck. Family. He called them a family and she rejoiced in the thought they could become a permanent unit. She carried the artwork from the house and stowed the two pieces in the front passenger seat. The temperature had risen several degrees. Delicate snowflakes fluttered from the air. She held the sides of her coat close together and glanced into the gray overcast sky. At one time she loved to play in the snow, creating angels and smashing icy-balls together to throw at her cousins.

She'd teach Justin how to make a snow fort if … Would they stay with Morgan in Cyan? Should she plan on going back to Briarwood? Outside of mentioning an "engagement" in Monsieur Barrett's office and the loose use of fiancée at the cottage, not another word had been spoken of their future. Should she bring up the topic? What if he had been trying to help her, as he always did, and wasn't sincere? She'd initiate an awkward situation if she introduced the subject of expectations or marriage.

"What are you daydreaming about?"

She lowered her face, from skyward, and met Beck's stare. What could he possibly want? "I thought you went back to Briarwood."

Justin would be getting up from his nap. She didn't want any sort of confrontation around him. Her breath caught. She didn't want Justin to be told Morgan wasn't his father. She bit her bottom lip and pushed her hand against her stomach, trying to stop the cramping and twisting.

"I couldn't leave without wishing you luck." His face was hard, jaw tight with a vibration twitching on the lower left side. Icy blue eyes narrowed and bits of anger glinted from their shallow depths. Before he went to Iraq he used to smile including his eyes. The three or four times she'd talked to him in the past year, melancholy or rage seemed to be his usual expressions.

"Luck?" She smiled and moved her hand from her belly. Her first love would always remain a part of her history, despite his refusal to acknowledge their past relationship. Beck remained in the past. Morgan was steadfastly planted in her present and God willing, her future.

"I remember everything, Shania." Beck stepped closer to her.

She jumped back, hoping he hadn't noticed her quivering arms, and placed both shaking hands on her stomach to hold in the spasms. "Regarding?"

"You never wrote to me once. I wonder why?" He gripped her arm and pulled.

"Odd, I thought you had Shania-amnesia." Flippancy hadn't been a part of her character until now, but she hit the target.

He narrowed his eyes. A low growl came from his throat.

"You never wrote to me. Not one letter or sexy telephone connection." Angry hard hitting words rang through the air.

"I never received a message from you, so how could I have a return address?" She jerked her arm from his and pushed away. "Strange behavior, for a devoted fiancé, don't you think?"

He snarled, then continued as if she hadn't made the last comment. "At first, I received regular updates from Morgan. He let you live almost rent-free in his house. Did you trade sex for rent?"

"No." Her mind whirled. "I sent the check to an LLC."

Morgan owned the little house on Beeker. Beck had known she was desolate and never contacted her? Her tiny bit of love for Beck leaked, leaving an open fissure behind.

"He helped deliver my son. Don't give me that surprised look. Justin resembles me. His attitude is exactly like yours. From what I understand, he's gifted with my talent." A slight smile appeared on his face and disappeared as fast as the lacy flakes of snow melting in the warm air. "I knew our children would be unusual."

"Your parents will never, ever, get him, Beck. Your name isn't on the birth certificate. The Longviews do not exist to him," she spat. She pivoted, started toward the house.

"He's only marrying you because of the vow."

Shania stopped, dead, and turned. Her heartbeats, pulsing in her throat, halted. "What?"

"You remember. I made my best friend, Morgan, swear he'd take care of you until I was able to do so again. He asked you to marry him out of pity. He thinks I won't remember. I do." His tick jumped faster, his eyes sparkled with glee.

"It's none of your business what I do with my life, Beck." She swallowed the bile in her throat, pivoted and demurely hurried to the cottage.

"Wait," he coaxed.

She stilled.

Beck's tone lowered, almost becoming a whine. "Wait for me to come…"

Oh God, he was her client, S1287. He'd called, talked to her through Companion Connections for the past year. He requested she say naughty things. As a result of the extended amount of phone time she'd been able to quit the job and go to school full-time. Did he know she was Shay?

Unable and unwilling to turn around, she grasped the door handle. A quick shove and she'd be inside, away from him.

"To you. Shania, I did send you letters, to your parents' address."

"You're not a part of our lives, Beck. Leave us alone." She rushed inside and shut and locked the door. So cold. She wrapped the coat close to her numb skin. A quick glance at Justin, asleep on the sofa, proved he was quiet and unaware of the upheaval. The destruction of her hopes and dreams.

A cartoon darted across the television screen. The alphabet song filled the room as the character sang. Shania shuffled to the air register. She stood on top of the metal grate, allowing the heat to slide up her legs and enter her system.

Her research in the university library validated PTSD didn't erase memories, which was the problem. The victims want to get rid of the horror, the visions of their past. Beck knew while denying her and Justin's existence. He'd always remembered her, so why had he contradicted the knowledge?

Had Shania's parents kept Beck's letters? No, Beck lied. He never sent correspondence. How would he benefit by lying?

The answer: Because Beck actually didn't want to marry her. He hadn't believed her son was his. What had changed? Why did he want to acknowledge Justin? She bit her lip. The Longviews had been notified of Justin's gift. They could get a lot of publicity from being tied to a three-year-old artistic genius. She wouldn't allow Beck to further a possible political career by using Justin. Morgan would protect his son.

The ringing cellphone brought her out of her musings. She dug the sleek device out of her rear pocket as she walked to the front door to look outside. "Hello."

Beck had left. She trotted back to the heater. Justin stirred, his eyelids fluttering.

"Shania, it's Monsieur Barrett. I'm excited to tell you I've taken Justin's artwork to a gallery in The Village, on Thistle Down Street. Do you remember we talked about the prestigious gallery?" His voice vibrated as he rushed the words.

Justin's sleepy blue-green eyes stared at her.

She lowered her voice. "I'm sorry I don't. Are the Longviews involved in the gallery in any way, even as a silent partner?"

"No. The owner, Jim Caraway, is on the advisory board for Briarwood's museum, but he is not associated in his private business with the Longviews. I said I'd let him know within the hour. Are you willing to let me showcase Justin's work?" His breathless voice stopped. Silence ensued.

Justin slid off the sofa and toddled down the hallway.

Her mind shouted no, but her spirit protested. Her son's genius should be viewed by others. Even the still-life of a peach he'd created. "Yes."

"You and Justin need to be at the gallery one week from Tuesday at six sharp," he exclaimed. "Need I tell you to dress as a professional?"

He was rude and insulting--she knew which garments were appropriate for a gallery showing. "Why so soon?"

"He had an opening at the last minute. Since Justin's work is on a small scale he's exhibiting the two pieces." The sound of rough, dry hands rubbing together transmitted through the phone.

"Right. We'll be there." She disconnected. The sound of water being splashed came from the guest bath. She walked down the hallway and leaned against the frame of the open door. Justin rubbed his hands together creating bubbles, and then smacked his palms. Clouds of soap rose into the air. She smiled. "Want a snack?"

"Crunch?" he asked and yawned. She'd given him a bath before his nap. Short fuzz lifted on one side of his head.

She placed her fingers in the water, testing the temperature. "Rinse off your hands. I'll get you a peach, because soon we're going to dinner."

Her wet fingers worked through his short locks, smoothing down the hair. He played in the water for a few more minutes, and then they walked into the kitchen. She helped him onto a stool and tucked a towel into his shirt, hoping the cloth would absorb the drops of water.

He grabbed the cotton and pulled.

"The towel will keep your shirt clean. You won't have to change again." She tugged the cloth farther down.

He quirked an eyebrow as if thinking about it, probably deciding how much more time he'd have to play if a change wasn't in the equation. "Okay."

She lifted a peach from the counter. Her stomach churned as she peeled off the skin. A moment later she considered calling Barrett and cancelling. Her fingers scooped out the pit before slicing the flesh. She didn't want Justin's art to be placed in a show, drawing more undesirable attention. As she placed bright orange-yellow slices on a plate she reconsidered. Shania Miller always honored her agreements. She grabbed the jug of milk from the fridge and filled the sippy-cup.

The snack prepared, she set the dish in front of Justin and handed him a fork. Shania picked up toys and cleaned the kitchen as he ate the peach and drank his milk.

"Are you done?" she asked as he scooted to the edge of the chair.

"Yes. Can I watch TV?"

"Yes, good idea. You watch a program, and I'll shower. Then we'll go to Morgan's parents' house." Shania flipped on the television and a blue fuzzy monster popped out of a trash can.

"See horses?" he asked as he lowered to sit on the carpet.

"Probably not tonight, Justin."

He frowned and focused on TV as a big yellow bird plastered across the entire screen.

She smoothed his hair. "If the bell rings or if anyone knocks just watch TV. Do not open any door and let someone inside."

Her voice must have held a hint of fear because his eyes became round.

"Okay, Mommy."

She kissed his forehead. "I'll shower and be right back."

Shania didn't believe Beck would return, but she didn't plan to put her son at risk. She bit her lip as she walked into the bedroom. Her queasy stomach didn't help her nerves to settle. She wanted to make a positive impression on Morgan's parents. Despite having known them for the past four years, this dinner would be different. She was in love with Morgan and wanted them to see her as…what? A daughter-in-law?

Excitement pattered a snappy beat inside her as she stepped into the tiled stall shower. Being with Morgan for the rest of her life would be a dream come true. She pressed her hands to her face. Yes, she hoped Morgan's parents would call her daughter. She desperately wanted to be part of a family again.

She practiced what she would say as she ran the razor over her legs and underarms. The day she'd bought Justin a ball she'd purchased a tube of quality lipstick, facial moisturizer, Included was a bonus sample bottle of bath wash and lotion. The decadent scent reminded her of berries and jasmine. A hint of vanilla relaxed her. What was Beck's intent?

Out of the shower she wrapped a towel around her, then bent in half shaking the hairs to maximize volume with her hair dryer. Upright again, she towel blotted her skin and finished by smearing lotion on her arms, neck and legs. Undergarments in place, she slipped into a black cowl-neck dress. The cotton top was form fitting, but the bottom flared like a large flexible umbrella. She forced her legs into pantyhose, but the toes rebelled when stuffed into black high heels. Her grandmother's pearls were placed in her ears.

"I want to wear my boots," Justin said. He held the rodeo riders lassoing straight forward. The towel was missing from around his neck, the shirt remained clean.

"Wouldn't you rather wear the shoes that light?" She applied her lipstick in the mirror, resisting the urge to smile as he frowned.

"No, I want to wear boots."

She faced him."I'd rather you wear the sneakers."

"Boots," he demanded.

"All right, if you can put your boots on the right feet, then you can wear them."

Her cellphone rang, interrupting any further rebellion. "Hello."

Justin sat on the floor, a thoughtful expression on his face. The cowboys swinging their ropes on leather rested beside him.

"Hi, I'm sorry about being gone most of the afternoon. I'm about ten minutes out of town. Could we drive separately? I'll meet you there," Morgan said. A horn honked in the background, with wheels squealing against the pavement.

"Sounds like you're in a street race."

"Crazy drivers. I'll see you there. Okay?"

"Sure. We'll see you there." She hung up and glanced at Justin. "While you're trying on your boots, I'll get our coats."

"Okay, is this right?" He had one shoe in place, the toe pointed outward.

She didn't want him to wear the oversized, noisy footwear but she admired his determination.

"No, honey, wrong foot." She left the room as he removed them.

She obtained Justin's coat from the closet and lifted her jacket off the rack in the foyer. Clomp, clomp vibrated on the hardwood floors behind her. She pivoted to look at him.

"Congratulations." Shania smiled at him. She removed the bunch of multi-colored hot-house flowers from the refrigerator. The fall fresh-scented champagne roses, fern leaves and chrysanthemums reminded her of fun times at school dances and family gatherings complete with winter centerpieces.

She placed the flowers beside her coat on the back of the sofa. Justin struggled to get his arms in his jacket. After assisting him and with mitts and hat in place, he was ready to go. Covering herself with her wool wrap, she picked up the flowers and her purse. A quick visual check over the living room indicated the interior was tidy, except for a couple of stray toys.

"Let's go, cowboy." She hoisted her bag onto her shoulder and took Justin's hand into hers.

The snow continued to flow, lightly covering her car and the ground. Beautiful flakes placed a pristine blanket on the evening ahead.

* * * *

Morgan answered the door, wet hair flipping onto his forehead. He'd dressed in an emerald shirt, bringing out the glorious moss green of his eyes. Jeans and boots finished off the outfit. His light peck to her lips warmed them the slightest bit.

"Sorry, I'm so late. I've got great news," Shania said to Morgan. She lowered two framed sketches to the slate of Hardwick's entrance hall floor, propping them against the staircase. Tucking the bunch of flowers under her arm, she helped Justin remove his coat. His gloves littered the floor. Out of the garment, he stood to the side, replicating Morgan's usual stance. Hands in his pockets, Justin rocked heel to toe.

"I was worried," Morgan responded and moved behind her. She shrugged. His fingers touched her neck as the jacket was removed, igniting that slow burn. She switched the chrysanthemum-laden floral bouquet from one hand to another as she moved her arms through the sleeves.

"Daddy." Justin tugged on Morgan's pant leg. "Mommy wouldn't let me wear boots."

Morgan lifted Justin and hooked Shania's coat on the stair rail. "It looks like you're wearing them."

Justin's frown turned upside down. "Uh-huh."

"Oh good, we'll get started with dinner now that the guest of honor is here." His mother, deep green eyes glittering, entered the foyer. Mark followed a step behind.

"Mom." He shifted Justin to his other side and hugged Shania to his side. "You remember Shania Miller, and this young man is Justin."

Shania held out the bunch of flowers. "It's a pleasure to see you again, Mrs. Hardwick, and Mark. I'm sorry we're late." She handed the spray to his mother, as she'd rehearsed during the shower.

"That's okay, dear, remember you were going to call me Maggie." Mrs. Hardwick took the bouquet, gave Shania a hug, and glanced at Justin. "Hi, Justin. Are you hungry?"

"Don't stand out here in the foyer, come. Welcome, Shania and Justin." Mark took Shania's arm and pulled her forward into the formal dining room off the foyer.

Shania stopped in her tracks. Her heart raced as fast as the sixty miles per hour she'd driven the last ten miles. She licked her lips, and slid her palms against the cold cotton of her dress. At least the sweat palm prints wouldn't show on the black material.

A white linen cloth covered an eight-foot table, showcasing stoneware place settings. The formality of the table arrangement didn't bother her, but the people made her palms hotter and damper. Patty, Morgan's ex-fiancée, sat beside Too Many, and then Shania's father. Shania's mother held court across from her father. Anger ripped through her like tearing a poorly created sketch, heating her core. Damn, this was a horrible set-up. She bit her lip and glanced at Morgan.

A broadcast smile lit his face.

He'd arranged this atrocity.

The chair beside her mother hosted a booster seat, which meant Shania had to sit beside Justin in the uncomfortable triangle. Her stomach soured with anger. The fury roiled to her throat, making it burn. They hadn't believed her about only being with Beck, and then demanded she abort her baby. She couldn't get over their mistrust. She shot Morgan a death-to-you-look.

Morgan winked in return.

Shania understood why Too Many was there. He was Morgan's friend. But why would he possibly invite that witch Patty? Unless Too Many had scooped-up Morgan's leftovers. Her parents? What could he possibly be thinking inviting her blood relations to share a meal with them?

"Sorry, we're late. Hello, Patty, Too Many, Father and Mother." Shania turned to take Justin from Morgan.

Instead of giving Justin to her, Morgan placed her baby on the seat. He pointed to her parents. "Justin, this is your grandmother and grandfather."

"Holy crap," Justin announced and glanced at her for confirmation. Shania nodded.

Mark softly chuckled. Too Many snorted.

Morgan held her seat beside Justin and across from Too Many. She flashed Morgan a questioning frown and slid onto the chair. He half-smiled, but his eyes held a ripple of uncertainty. He settled onto the ladder-back next to her and shook his napkin.

Shania lifted a piece of fabric and tried to place the soft blue material on Justin's lap.

"Shania, if you don't mind we have a toy truck for your son--Justin," her mother declared.

The gift didn't surprise Shania, but she found the opening comment odd. No "hello, how have you been" or "why did you ruin your life?" However, her mother's fingers shook as she creased a section of her navy napkin.

"Truck," Justin shouted and moved to get off the seat.

Shania placed her hand on his. "After dinner. Everyone's been waiting on us."

He kicked his boots against the frame of the seat and tossed his napkin to the floor.

"Those are nice boots, Justin," her mother said, trying to win him over. Shania's mother was a professional. The experience from numerous charity events would enable her to convince King Midas himself to give up his gold and join the cause. No doubt by complimenting Justin's footwear and giving a gift she'd get his favor in no time.

Justin smiled and raised a leg, bumping into the bottom of the table. Mrs. Hardwick had placed dishes on the center and as they rattled, she glanced at him. He thumped the wood again. She held onto the gravy boat with two hands.

"Sister M said..." Justin stammered and held his shoe out for examination and praise.

"What did Sister M say?" her mother urged, sending him a reassuring smile.

Oh, no!

"They were slightly used." Justin smiled. He was proud as can be of his boots, and kicked the wood as he slid his foot under the table.

Heat rushed up to Shania's face. She reached over and pushed down the leg, so he wouldn't jar the table again. "Justin, shh."

"Robert, did you hear that?" her mother whispered across the table.

"We all heard him, Mrs. Hardwick," Patty's spiteful voice spewed. A devilish smile followed.

Shania lowered her face, willing the heat to recede.

"A moment of prayer, please," Mr. Hardwick announced. He quoted scripture, added a note about guests, and ended. "Peace be with you."

"As with you," Mrs. Hardwick, Morgan and Shania said in unison.

Much to Shania's amazement, the meal continued without further incident. Limited conversation had been bantered about other than a couple of fishing tales. Justin spilled a few kernels. Yellow corn edged the tablecloth around his plate. He ate more than he had in the past few weeks. Was another growth spurt coming?

He held his tiny hand to her face and whispered, "Can I get down?"

Shania glanced at Morgan. "Sure," Morgan replied.

"Shania, would it be all right if we gave Justin his gift?" Her mother rubbed her aging hand over Justin's smooth small one. A look of poignant longing appeared on her face. Almost four years had passed since Shania had seen her mother and father. Her parents had aged with lines creasing their faces, saggy jaws and stomachs that flopped over their belts. Had they kept Beck's letters? No, she wouldn't believe it. Beck had lied.

"Truck." Justin glowed. Having forgotten about the prize, now he couldn't wait to leave.

Shania glanced at Morgan. "Is there a place he could play with a toy?"

"Kitchen?" Morgan glanced at his mother.

"Sure. Justin, the kitchen floor is made from bricks. You'll enjoy running a truck over the rough terrain, like in the desert." Mrs. Hardwick smiled at him, lifting and lowering her hand in a wave motion, imitating a vehicle on an uneven road.

"Do you need to use the restroom before you go play?" Shania helped him down from the seat.

He squinted, hesitated, and a quick nod followed.

Bathroom activities done, her mother took Justin's hand and led him to the kitchen. A wrapped rectangle secure under her arm. Shania experienced a spasm of pain in her chest. The past was the past. She shouldn't deny her son his family. By coming here tonight her parents flung out the olive branch, and she'd embrace the offering. Justin would get to know his grandparents.

Shania relaxed and settled onto her seat. Morgan placed his arm around her shoulders.

"Since we're going to have a special announcement during dessert, I thought we'd have home-made ice cream to go with the cake. Morgan, would you go out to the garage to get the ice from the freezer?" Mrs. Hardwick asked and nodded toward the door.

"I'll be happy to." He kissed Shania's cheek and whispered, "I'll be right back."

Shania's mother came from the kitchen and called her father. He excused himself from the table. They walked into the living room.

Great, Justin probably told her about PBJs for dinner a few nights ago.

"Since we have some time until the big announcement, I'll get a drink. A real drink." Patty got up and walked into the kitchen.

What was the big announcement? Was Too Many marrying Patty? The moment Patty's short skirt snaked past the door, Shania shot a glance at Too Many. He hadn't tied two words together the entire night.

"What are you thinking, getting mixed up with her?" Shania squeezed out and then glanced at Mark, the only other person at the table. He calmly sipped coffee as he stared a set of bay windows at the other end of the room.

"What can I say? I like bad women." He smiled and lifted his glass, as if toasting her.

"I'm not a bad woman. At one time I thought I loved Beck. Morgan is my true love and that doesn't make me...like her." She didn't care if Too Many thought she was wicked. Only Morgan's opinion mattered.

"Of course you're not bad. If you were, I'd have hit on you a long time ago." Too Many grinned.

A shriek pierced the silence.

"Justin!" Shania jumped from her chair and ran into the kitchen. The swinging door banged against the wall and remained in place, stuck on the clasp to hold it secure.

"You little bastard," Patty screamed.

Justin grabbed his large yellow metal truck off Patty's elegant designer shoe and backed up like a sand crab.

"You need to train your bastard brat." Patty lifted her shoe and brushed at the leather.

Shania lifted Justin and held him on her hip. She shoved his head to her shoulder, covering the exposed ear with her hand.

"You can say whatever you want to me, but I will *not* allow you to call my son hurtful names." Shania's breath came fast, expanding her chest. Surely Justin's head moved with the pounding.

"Bitch, whore, man stealer, what else do you want to hear? You're more than that." Patty's breathing took on a fast pace as well. She'd apparently been gathering steam in the past three months.

"You weren't meant to be together. He didn't love you, Patty." Shania held her hand tighter to Justin's ear.

"And he does you? Can't you see what's in front of you? For the past four years he's been kowtowing to you because Beck asked him too. Morgan's the kind of guy who takes his obligations seriously. So many times we couldn't take a vacation or even go to a movie because he was on call for you. He's not in love with you. Morgan's fulfilling a vow he made to his best friend," Patty harped.

"Patty," Too Many protested from behind Shania.

Shania turned to leave. Regardless of how much she disliked Patty, she was right. Beck had said the same thing. Morgan would honor a vow. He'd do whatever he promised and for however long it took to protect her and Justin.

She released her hand from Justin's head. Tears blinded her as she pushed past Too Many. Her parents were walking back into the dining

j.j. Keller

room. "Justin, tell your grandmother and grandfather 'thank you' for the truck."

"Thank you," he whimpered, then suctioned his head to her shoulder.

Shania blinked away the tears and glanced around the room. "Thank you, Mark, for dinner. Please tell Mrs. Hardwick the food was delicious. I'll call Morgan."

Morgan's father stared at her as if trying to decide what she was saying. They must not get a lot of squabbling at their house. He lifted his coffee cup and nodded.

She lowered Justin to the floor and grabbed his coat from the wooden staircase banister. With quick rough movements she took the toy and placed it on the tile. She tucked his arms into the coat and zipped it rapidly enough the teeth-gathering echoed through the small foyer. Morgan came around the corner as she jerked on her wrap. Justin picked up his truck, holding it close to his chest and backed into her legs.

"What's going on?" Morgan moved his glance between her and Justin. Shania's hands trembled as she tried to secure one edge over her shoulder. He wrapped his arms around her. "Tears? Why?"

She sniffed, stepped away, and wiped her face with her sleeve.

"We're leaving. Got to get back." She chuckled, trying to keep the hysteria out of her voice. Reluctant to depart, she couldn't stay knowing he'd commit to her because of loyalty. As many times as he'd hinted about love, he'd never said the words.

"I thought you were staying over?" He glanced at the people nearby. "Give us a moment."

Their audience crept back into the dining room.

"Why are you running away again?" he growled.

Justin moved to her side and hung onto the hem of her jacket.

"I'm not running. I was going to call you." She took Morgan's hand, cleared her throat, and licked her lips. She loved him, enough that she'd release him. "Morgan, when I didn't have anyone to lean on, you were there for me. You provided me with lodging, comfort and a shoulder to cry on. You obliged me by going with me to doctor visits and in helping to deliver my son. I depended on you and still do depend on you. You have always been there for me, but it was because you made a vow to Beck before he left for the military. Remember, I was there. 'I promise to take care of Shania until you're able to once again,'" she quoted and then sniffed. "You didn't realize it'd be a life sentence, did you?"

* * * *

"Shania, that's not all true." Morgan's mind raced trying to sort out why she was running away and in tears. What had happened? Her demeanor had changed. She stood straight as if a rod had been inserted in her back. Her pale face had a stream of tears cascading. Justin clung to her. His chest hurt because he might lose them, and he didn't know why.

"Shh, let me finish. When I left for Briarwood I was scared. So afraid I'd fail. Fail at school and fail at taking care of Justin. Would we survive? Had I saved enough?" She half-smiled. "We *are* doing okay. We buy used clothing and eat cheap meals, but we're doing okay. And do you know what?"

"No, what?" His voice came out husky with emotion. Tears dripped from her chin. He wanted to grab her and shake her into understanding their love would last forever. Whatever had happened they could work through it together.

"Even after I thought you'd married I continued to put your name as primary contact in case of emergency, because I knew you'd be there for us." She wiped her face. "I'm letting you go. You've completed your obligations to Beck, Morgan Hardwick. You are free. Go marry that bitch if you want, take a cruise, because your vow has been fulfilled."

Shania Miller, the love of his life, picked up their son and walked out the door. His entire future sizzled, fluttered and fell to the floor. This time he would run after her.

Patty slammed the door shut and grabbed his arm.

Morgan would damn well find out why she left, and then surpass speed limits to catch her.

Chairs screeched across the wooden floor as the others joined them in the foyer.

"What happened here? I was gone five minutes getting ice and came back to…"

All eyes took a keen interest in the tile floor, except his father's.

"Dad, why did my future bride run out the door?"

"Son, I want you to know I'll be proud to call her my daughter." He glanced around the empty foyer. "And that boy is something else."

"Yes, I agree. Tell me what happened." Morgan had to find out the reason so he could make it right.

His father sighed. "That woman went into the kitchen." He nodded toward Patty. "A few minutes later we heard caterwauling and Shania ran inside, leaving the door open. Justin calls you Daddy?"

"Yes, I'm the only male adult he's been around. It's natural. Besides, I am his daddy."

Patty snickered. He glowered at her.

His father pointed his thumb at Patty. "She called your son a bastard. Shania said to call her names, but not her son. That woman did and said you didn't love Shania. You were fulfilling your vow to Beck." He paused and stared at Morgan. "I'm glad you didn't marry *her.*" He glanced at Patty. "Now, go bring Shania and Justin home to us."

"I will, Dad. I plan to make a half-dozen more kids with her." He smiled.

"Morgan, she was a call girl, a whore, for Companion Connections," Patty screamed.

Mrs. Miller gasped and started forward. Mr. Miller stopped her.

Morgan flipped his hand over and pushed down. "Not a whore. She answered calls."

"As far as you know," she spewed.

"I do know. Tom and I own Companion Connections. I gave her the job, and I own the house she lived in. My promise to Beck was made because I loved her. Reflecting back, I think he knew it as well. I'll always love her. I don't love you, Patty, and now, I don't even like you." Morgan switched his attention to Shania's parents.

"Companion Connections was originally designed to help older individuals who have no family or treated their family members poorly and do not have contact with them. They need conversations. Lonely people seek companionship. Most men wish for some zing during their phone call, but they are disconnected if they get beyond a certain point. For the past three and a half years, Shania was one of the listeners for those lonely souls. She earned and saved her money. When she couldn't continue to take distance-learning classes, she left and started attending the university full-time. I invited you here tonight to witness my engagement to Shania. I love your daughter. The past is the past, but I hope you don't become one of those lonely people. As far as I'm concerned, what happened between you and her years ago has been buried. You're welcome to attend the wedding." He took a breath, wanting to get on the road. She'd probably already finished packing and would be leaving his house.

"Yes, we'll be at the wedding," Mr. Miller stated.

"Anything else we need to get aired?" Morgan asked.

"Go get your girl," his father said.

Morgan pulled the door open and ran. He stopped in front of her car. The lights were on and the motor rumbled into the night. His heart tapped against his chest as fast as the thunking of the pistons.

Shania lay on the ground, unmoving. Morgan dropped beside her and gently turned her over. Blood dripped from her forehead, coating her hair.

"Shania." He supported her shoulders, then touched his fingers to her neck. She had a pulse--a slow one, but she was alive.

A flood of outside lights flashed on and his father shouted, "Morgan, you forgot your keys."

"Dad, call nine-one-one." He slowly lowered her to the ground, noticing one of Justin's boots and the yellow truck nearby.

His father's heavy breathing arrived before he did.

"Good Lord, what has happened?" Mark knelt, pried the area round her wound, and lifted her eyelids. "We need to get her to a hospital. The injury isn't that deep, but she's not coming around."

Morgan jerked open the back passenger door and shouted, "Justin?" Morgan fell against the unforgiving metal. "He's gone. Beck. Beck took him."

Chapter 17

Morgan paced the cold, sterile hospital corridor outside Shania's room. Quick, long steps, ten down and twelve for the return. One of his weaknesses was waiting. He had no tolerance for delays. He glanced at the police detectives interviewing his mother and father. What the hell was taking so long? The cops needed to hunt down Beck and return Justin before Shania woke.

Patty's foul disposition and greed had been the final straw. She probably had arranged to create a distraction allowing Beck the chance to disable Shania and grab Justin. Patty wanted to hurt him. Nobody was to blame except him—he gave Patty the chance to slander Shania. He brought the group together last night, knowing Tom was dating Patty. Idiot! She carried a grudge. Morgan's focus always remained on Shania. His guard was down.

He inhaled, and blew out the air. The scents of the hospital--cleaning fluid, blood and starched lab coats--brought happy memories of Justin's birth fresh into his mind. Morgan's mind replayed the day his son was born.

* * * *

"Isn't he beautiful, Morgan?" Shania's sweat had matted her hair and her cheeks were red from pushing the baby out of a very large hole. He hadn't wanted to watch. As Shania's coach, he only had to keep her mind focused on regulated breathing. The lights were bright and mirrors were everywhere. His gaze continued to return to the miracle of birth.

Morgan edited the comments running through his head and tried to calm his tumultuous stomach. "Yes, he is beautiful."

And ringing through his mind was, he should have been my son.

"What should we call him?" She acted as if he'd continue to be a part of the child's life. Morgan rejoiced in the fact that she wanted him to be.

He'd loved her at first sight and four years later he respected her, admired her and had become friends with her. He wanted more, but did she?

"What do you think of Justin? I've always liked the name. It's Latin in origin, and means upright and righteous. There was a Saint Justin who wrote the moral values of Christianity." He smoothed the hair back from her forehead, and then touched the sprinkles of golden locks on the baby's head as he rested, bundled in a blue blanket and tucked close to her chest.

"I like the name Justin. Justin Miller. Has a nice ring to it." She gazed into his eyes. "I didn't realize you were so religious."

"Not a Bible toter, but I believe in faith, hope and love." He sat on the edge of the bed, exhausted from the last forty-eight hours. He didn't want to leave because he'd have to face Patty. They'd been en route to the airport heading for a vacation in Jamaica. Patty threatened to break up with him, in the airport parking lot, if he left to go to "that woman."

A nurse walked into the room with a clipboard in hand. "Miss Miller, I need you to fill out this paper work to get your little guy registered and a birth certificate created."

"By law do I have to put the father's name on the birth certificate?" She held Justin close to her chest. He'd woken. His blue eyes wide opened. He puckered his mouth and air bubbles formed. Even when Justin's eyes became blue-green, they continued to stare at Morgan as if he were the most important person, other than his mother, in his life.

"No, you do not have to list the father's name." She flipped through some pages on her clipboard. "Here is an information document from our social work department which explains a variety of situations. You can always talk to a social worker or your attorney." She glanced at Morgan and patted Shania's hand. "I'll collect the paper later." The nurse left the room

Shania's hand couldn't hold the document. Morgan took it from her and after a couple of minutes he said, "Bottom line, if you do put the baby's father's name on the birth certificate and the father acknowledges paternity, he'd have rights. He could get parenting time. However, you could get child support as well."

"Morgan, although Beck is the biological father, I don't want his manipulative family to have access to Justin. Do you think sometime in the future, I'll regret not putting his name on the form?"

"The decision has to be yours, Shania. I assume you could add Beck's name later." He placed the paper on a side table, took the baby from her arms, and cradled him. Morgan shoved the resentment deep down. "When you get married."

White-knuckled, she held the clipboard in her hands. "What if Beck doesn't come back?" Tears clouded her eyes. "He's never contacted me, and now he's been taken by rebels."

"Don't get excited about something you can't control." His voice was soft, but anger toward Beck stirred like an ugly monster in his stomach, mixing up the bile.

She grabbed a tissue and wiped her tears. "Thinking of the worst case scenario, what if he doesn't return? His mother would find a way of altering Justin's birth certificate to meet her needs. She has people everywhere to do her bidding."

"You could put my name as the father." Gallant, he offered his surname as if her using his name on a legal document identifying her son as his wasn't the most important event in his life to date. In reality he wanted to have his name attached to her baby more than drawing breath. His strongest desire was to be the one responsible, to have Shania and Justin as a part of his life forever. Morgan drew in the fresh scent of the babe. As he talked, the infant's eyes opened and the newborn snuggled closer. Did his son recognize his voice?

* * * *

"Code blue, four north." The announcement came from overhead. Morgan shook off the memory of Justin's birth, stopped pacing, and took a drink from the water fountain. Morgan never regretted the decision to claim Justin as his own and he would become a Hardwick. He planned to marry Shania and adopt Justin as soon as this crisis ended and he could talk some sense into her pretty pixie head.

"Morgan?" Mr. Miller touched his shoulder, bringing him further back to time and place.

"What did you find out? What did the doctor say?" Morgan swiped a hand through his hair. They'd been in the hospital waiting area for eleven hours getting sporadic information.

"She's still in coma." Mr. Miller nodded to a grouping of chairs ten steps away. "Why don't you sit for a spell?"

"I can't. I must do something. The police don't seem to acting on this."

"They have people scouring the woods. There isn't evidence that Beck took Justin."

"He didn't wander away. Justin's a smart kid. He would have gotten help for her."

Mr. Miller scratched the day old whiskers on his face. "You still believe Beck took him?"

"I know he did. Regardless of what the Longviews claim, Beck took my son." Morgan glanced through the window. Shania's head was wrapped in a white bandage nearly blending in with her skin. Bright red clown cheeks proved she'd gotten a fever. He turned, needing to find a nurse who could give her aspirin and maybe an antibiotic.

His cellphone rang to the tune *You're the One*. "Excuse me, I need to take this."

Mr. Miller nodded and went into Shania's room.

Morgan pushed the door open and walked onto the staircase landing. "Justin?"

"Daddy?" Justin's voice quivered over the phone. Somehow Justin had gotten a hold of Shania's phone and had successfully kept it from his kidnapper.

Morgan could imagine Justin's tiny lip shaking. "Yes, son, I'm here. Tell me where you are, and I'll come get you."

"I don't know. The bad man hurt Mommy." Tears transcended the telephone wire, making Morgan's chest hurt. His eyes watered, clouding his vision.

"She's fine, a little bump on her head. She'll be better when she sees you." Morgan licked his dry lips and used the back of his hand to wipe away leakage. "Justin, where are you? Tell me what you see."

He sniffed. "Two beds, a bathroom--"

"Okay, son, where is Beck?" Morgan didn't need to ask who the bad man was.

"He went to get something to eat. I need you." A crying jag was just around the corner by the quivering in his voice.

"Justin, I'll come get you. I need to know where you are. Did the man say anything about where you were?"

"He said we'd be at the cabin tomorrow." Sniffles came through, pounding their sharp spikes into Morgan's gut.

"Good. Justin, look out the window and tell me what you see. Hurry."

The sound of a curtain shifting and then Justin's voice rang stronger than a moment before. "Cars, hills like on the painting Mommy did for her class, and a sign blinking."

"Super. Good. Can you tell me any of the letters on the sign?" Justin was soon to be four, but Morgan didn't know if he had any alphabet training.

"N. T. A. I. N. S.I." He drew in a sharp breath.

"What, Justin, tell me." Morgan's blood raced through his veins, making him dizzy. The stairwell door opened, and his father walked into the space with a questioning expression.

"The bad man is coming."

"Justin, hide your phone again. I'm coming for you. I'll be there as soon as possible. Son, do you remember when we went to buy your shoes and I was grumpy?"

"Yes," he whispered.

"Make the bad man take you to buy shoes. I'll have more time to get to you. I love you. I promise you, I'll be there to get you. Okay?"

"Okay, Daddy," he whispered.

The phone connection was lost.

"Beck has him?"

Morgan glanced at his father. "Yes, from what I could tell he's stopped at a hotel near the hills. They're headed toward the Longview's lodge. Beck must have forgotten I've seen photos of the cabin when he told me about their fishing trip."

"How did Justin call you?"

"He had Shania's phone. I'm guessing, logically, the hotel's called Mountainside. I'll do a search to verify. Could I borrow some of your weapons?" Morgan brought up his browser and searched.

"Yes. I'll come with you. I imagine you're rusty, and I've got combat training." He rubbed his hands together.

Morgan lifted an eyebrow. Combat training from fifty years ago. He confirmed the hotel's address and it was in line with his memory of the cabin's location. "It's urgent we leave now. How will I tell the cops? They'll restrain me for questions and a statement. I can't wait."

His mother came through the door. Three of them stood on the landing, no one ascending or descending the stairs.

"What's going on out here?"

Morgan glanced at his father and smiled.

Chapter 18

"Good thing Justin made a scene at the hotel about buying boots, so the clerk could give us a time they checked out," Mark said.

"Yes, at least now we have a time frame. If Justin was able to delay Beck by insisting on stopping for boots they've just arrived." Morgan snapped the barrel of the pistol into place. They had a small arsenal, including provisions for an overnight stay if needed.

"I have to admit when I saw the store with boots the size of Godzilla decorated in Christmas lights I was tempted to stop."

Morgan glanced at his dad. "We'll come back and you and Justin can shop. Are you certain we've parked far enough away from the cabin?"

"Yes."

They'd taken precious minutes to change into camouflage gear, which according to his father was needed to infiltrate.

He cut branches of nearby shrubs and covered the large square hood of the truck. They didn't take the time to hide the large bed in the back. Besides, the rust and green kind of blended in with the trees. The woody scent of evergreens and earth surrounded them.

"See, what did I tell you? The buggy has quiet power and got us over untried trails. We'll be closer for when we grab Justin. Faster getaway."

Morgan glanced at his father's face, slightly red from the exertion. "Our goal is to locate Justin. Hopefully we can take him away without gunfire. The cops are not going to be happy getting their intel second hand while we took control." He wiped a loose leaf from his forehead. "Justin was scared. I just want him to be safe. Hopefully, we'll be able to have him reunited with Shania as she wakes."

He thought of her lying pale and weak in a hospital bed and his chest pumped a fast as the whooshing of air through the pine trees.

"My recommendation is to head due south. Keeping in the perimeter, scout the area."

Morgan nodded. "Good idea, keep an eye on the windows to see if Justin is in one particular room."

"If he doesn't show, one of us will need to sneak inside. Do you think Beck hired people to guard them?" Mark pressed his shoulder hostler, tucking the leather under his arm. He shoved a hand into his pocket, jingling spare bullets.

"I doubt it, he's too arrogant. I'm going in. You'd be better as the sharpshooter if one is needed." Morgan sheathed a hunting knife and removed his locksmith kit. In case he needed to open a few doors, he withdrew a few picks and Ls.

"I'll go north, and we'll meet back in here, let's say in twenty minutes at ten thirty AM." Morgan glanced at the sun hidden behind thick gray clouds to get an idea of where they'd be most vulnerable.

"Go, we need to be quick. Get in and out before they realize something's up." Mark started walking with an agility Morgan hadn't seen in some time. No doubt his father felt at a loss without his practice. He probably wanted to keep busy, to feel needed. He had been very good with Justin.

"What do you think about starting a kid's camp in the west forest? Teach them how to survive in the wild?"

Mark smiled. "'Cause you did so well, I should teach others?"

"It took with me, but my interest went elsewhere. I've seen how you interact with Justin and the neighbor's three hoodlums. Children are relaxed around you. You could help them, make the kids feel empowered."

His father lifted an eyebrow, as if debating the idea. "We'll see."

They came to cross-paths. "You go that way. We'll meet back here in twenty. Do not talk on your cell. If something goes wrong, fire into the air."

The .38 special attached to his leg felt heavy. The weapons were a necessary evil, because if he had to, he'd drop and extract the gun. Reluctant to hurt another, he'd shoot into a body if necessary, whatever it took to get his son back. "Got it."

Morgan took off running, keeping on a deer trail. He finally saw the log cabin. Aged to a dark whiskey, the two-story structure stood out like a beacon in the afternoon light. Within range to see through the windows, he knelt behind an oak tree. He removed a pair of binoculars, as small as opera glasses. The images were fuzzy --but he didn't need more.

He struck a view in the upstairs room, getting only a sliver of the side of a person. The darkness inside failed to provide a true likeness. Morgan rolled the focus and repositioned on a window at the ground level, close to the front entrance. Beck's parents were sitting at a table. She held a short glass, half-filled with liquid. A frown marred her face. Mr. Longview pounded his hand on the table.

Morgan stepped to the other side of the tree. Lifting the binoculars he narrowed the lens on the next casement. Empty. Damn. He slipped the visual aid into his pocket. Jumping around tangled vines and sidestepping chuck holes, he jogged a few feet north to the next set of windows. One small pane and a transom, narrow and long. It wouldn't provide him a clue as to what was inside. He whipped the mini-telescopes from his pack and focused on the three-foot dormer. By the shower pipes above the curtain, it was a bathroom.

At the sound of a motor, he shifted to the side of the house. Mr. and Mrs. Longview were driving down the lane. Great, just what Morgan needed, for them to be out of the picture while he reclaimed his child. He held the binoculars in his hand and continued forward, scraping his hands as he shoved branches to the side. His breath stopped as he ground his feet in the tracks. The entire backside of the house was open apertures, rising twenty feet into sheltered tree lined sky. Morgan shoved the eyepiece to his face, picking up the shadowed outline of his father on the opposite side, a glimpse only. He was well hidden and wouldn't be noticed.

The stench of a dead animal made him gag. He covered his mouth. On a tiny trail was a half-eaten, partially decayed, small woodland creature. From the remains he couldn't determine if it was a raccoon or a groundhog. Five feet in front of him, a three trunked birch raised high into the air. The scaly white and grayish skin had shed, leaving its ruins on the ground. He glanced around the clearing near the house. The view would be perfect. He ran behind the trunk. His clothes blended with the colors, shielding him, providing an excellent view of the cabin.

Lifting the binoculars, he scanned the rooms from East to West. Movement appeared in the far corner, closest to his father. Morgan twisted the dials, drawing the profiles near, forcing them into fuzzy silhouettes. Because of size and shape he recognized Justin. He ran around a kitchen table, throwing bits of paper as he circled, acting as a three-year-old would but completely out of his own personal character. Beck threw open a door and shoved Justin onto the patio. Justin crossed his arms at his chest. The prospect of snow made the temperature damn cold and Beck forced the boy into the chilly morning air without a coat.

Morgan shoved the binoculars into his pocket and crept through the woods, getting closer to the terrace, hoping they would stay outside. He needed to take a risk and rescue his son.

"Listen, kid, you're in my care now and it's going to go my way or you're going to spend a lot of time under my hand." Beck smacked his palms together. Justin dropped to the deck. Falling onto wooden slats, wet leaves splat as his rear hit the surface. Murky spatters of mud shot into the air.

"I want my mommy."

"Tough, kid, your mommy's dead. Now get up, you're going to paint a picture for your Nanna and grandfather."

Justin's sobs rang through the trees, bouncing off the bark and echoing in the now totally overcast sky. Big fat tears rolled down his cheeks. Morgan wanted to rush forward to grab Justin and shoot the man holding him hostage. He didn't believe in violence, but he wanted to pierce Beck's heart with a bullet.

"Mommy's not dead, Daddy's coming to take me to her," Justin shouted and jumped to his feet. He took off running through the shrub border, directly in line with Mark. The boxwoods blocked Justin from view.

Beck shouted, "You brat, I am your fucking father." He walked to the edge of the bricks. "Get back here."

Morgan ran. Justin was fast, at least two yards in front of Beck. Justin disappeared into a line of white pine trees.

Beck swiveled, drawing a gun from the waistband in the groove of his back. He crouched, anticipating attack. Morgan didn't plan to disappoint him.

"Well, if it isn't the big bad businessman." Beck straightened to a firm stance.

"Drop the gun. Nobody needs to get hurt. We'll take Justin and leave." Morgan glanced at the trees, noticing a flash of light. Morris code. Damn, he wished he could remember the meaning of the dots and dashes.

"Regardless what the birth certificate says, he's my kid, not yours. He stays." Beck held the weapon in front of him, both hands gripping the handle.

"No, Justin's my son and I don't take it lightly when someone steals him from me." Morgan knelt and drew his .38 from the ankle holster. His aim was direct. His father taught him well: Shoot to kill.

Beck frowned, then scratched his chin. "The kid does look like your sister."

Morgan didn't say anything, focusing on Beck's face instead, waiting, watching for the slightest indication he'd shoot. Morgan needed to drag out the conversation, providing adequate time for his father to get Justin out of the area.

"You fucked her, didn't you? Did you think I hadn't noticed your attention to my girl, especially playing nursemaid when she got sick from the kegger." He waved the pistol. "That's when you banged her."

"The night you fucked the Cooke twins, you mean?"

Beck, the idiot, smiled. "I knew you'd screwed her. Sexiest voice I've ever heard. Called her at your little business, recorded our conversation. I replay it to beat off. I taught her, you know. She sucked at fucking, but once she learned how to talk dirty--"

"Shut-up!" Morgan fought the urge to damn him to hell. Shoot, his mind shouted. Instead he shoved the gun between his belt and camouflage pants. He stepped forward, and plowed his fist into Beck's face.

Beck went down, pistol waving. Before he hit the ground, he used his free hand to push upright.

As much as his instinct demanded he shoot, Morgan couldn't. "Justin's my child. Shania and I are getting married. I expect you to leave us alone. Don't come near either of them again."

Morgan turned. He closed his eyes and took a deep breath. Beck was a coward and wouldn't shoot. However, Beck actually went to boot camp. Morgan could very well be dead in the next few minutes.

Gunfire sounded. Morgan fell to the ground. He rolled, but didn't feel burning pain as he'd expected. His fingers clutched the handle of the pistol, trigger finger on the release. A trickle of blood formed on his left side. The river of crimson ran harder, faster, as he sat upright. He pointed his weapon in Beck's direction.

Boots landed heavy on the deck. A touch of brown came into his peripheral vision. "Sir, are you okay?"

"Yes." Morgan plopped onto the sod. The danger was over. Pain ripped through him. He glanced at his wound. A dark hole, almost perfect in shape, had gone through his jacket. Blood gushed onto the ground.

The cop leaned and threw Morgan's jacket back and lifted the shirt with the tip of his rifle. "Clean through." He touched the walkie-talkie on his shoulder holster. "Get the doctor up here. Man down and..."

He stepped forward, knelt beside Beck's inert body. Two fingers went to the neck. A few minutes passed and he said, "Another dead."

With unsteady hands Morgan lowered his cold gun. Sweat beaded his forehead. He had to ignore the dizziness and remain alert. His father would be worried. He had to be strong for Justin...and Shania. Darkness invaded.

* * * *

"Morgan?"

"Daddy?" Fingers shook his arm.

"Justin, be careful, Daddy has a needle in that arm."

Shania.

Starch and sterile scents of a hospital seeped into his nostrils.

She was awake. He wanted to open his eyes. Heavy. Pain burned into his side.

The crunch of the bed and movement brought milk-scented breath close. Moist lips touched his cheek, and then another larger set pressed against his forehead.

He lived. Shania had woken. Justin was safe with them. They were a family again.

Chapter 19

Shania propped her hand on the apartment doorframe, holding steady as she slipped on a cream-tinted heel.

"Justin, are you nervous?" Megan asked, at least for the third time.

"No." He tugged at his tie.

"Want to try the artist pose again?"

"No." He scooted, snug against the sofa's cushions.

"What's an artist pose?" Shania asked as she carefully migrated through the toys spread around the living room. She bent to collect a Matchbox car off the floor, wobbling as she did so. She'd worn flat shoes for so long she anticipated falling, from the gained height, straight onto her face.

"Show her, Justin," Megan persisted. Tonight her hair was black with crimson streaks. She claimed the color red was for good luck. However, the new shock of ruby also provided an excuse for a new piercing. A silver bar slid through her lower lip, with a garnet ball at the end.

"No." He crossed his arms.

"That's okay. Do you need to use the restroom before we go?" Shania asked. His grumpiness could have been a result of fussiness. Morgan hadn't contacted them for a few days. He recovered in record time from his injury, then resumed his active work schedule. Yesterday was to be his last hectic day. Vacation started today.

"No." Justin bounced his legs against the cushions.

Megan rolled her eyes.

A pout formed on his face.

"You don't have to talk, but you should be nice and smile." Shania walked to the mirror and placed her pearl earrings in her lobes.

"Will Daddy come?" Justin's voice held a hint of fear and sadness. Despite how much time passed since the incident at Morgan's parents' home, the kidnapping continued to bother him, keeping him up with nightmares. Last night he'd had another one, awaking twice thereafter from a restless sleep. Shania reassured him the bad man wouldn't get him again, and Morgan was his only father. Someday she'd have to explain the Longviews to Justin. She feared them petitioning for visiting rights, but Shania's attorney assured her that their involvement in the kidnapping would prevent them from ever being alone with him.

"Yes, honey. He said he'd be there." She swallowed the knot that caught in her throat thinking of the danger he'd put himself in to find Justin. Blinking back tears, she pivoted, pretending to smooth the silk dress. "Megan, thanks for arranging my hair. The fluffy fullness looks classy."

Megan cocked her head. "The style is perfect for hiding your scar."

Shania glanced at her. An angry frown marred her beautiful features. Megan threatened to cut Beck's testicles off, until Shania reassured her he'd never bother them again. "Will the curls stay like this all night?"

"Don't let your hunky man run his fingers through it, and you'll be fine." Megan laughed.

"Is your mother coming?" Shania removed Justin's new fleece jacket and her wrap from the coat rack. She tossed Justin's garment to Megan.

"She'll be late, but she'll be there. I'm taking photos." Megan caught Justin's coat. She coaxed him off the sofa, tickled him, and slipped his arms into the dark blue sleeves. Clever.

Shania anticipated the cream-tinted wrap on top of an off-white dress would be a mistake. One sticky hand print from Justin, and she'd have a stain for the rest of the night. Yet she couldn't resist buying the garment. According to Megan, the light material made her skin appear pearl in tone, with a slight blush showing from underneath. Megan helped her apply makeup to enhance the essence. Shania's queasy stomach rumbled. Would she embarrass herself by vomiting?

She pulled on her gloves. An exhale didn't ease her anxiety. "I'm a little nervous."

"Do you feel sick?" Megan asked.

"You promised you'd take me to buy a Christmas tree," Justin whined.

"Yes, I told you I would and I will." She kissed his cheek. "I'm not sick. I'm excited for you."

He frowned. She'd upset him.

"I'm really excited for people to see your artwork." She shot him a smile.

"I'll show you," he declared.

Shania glanced at him. Show her what?

He shoved his tiny chin into the air, side-view, head tossed back, and tucked a hand on his hip, with his other palm upright, elbow bent.

Shania chuckled. Megan chortled.

"I'm not so nervous now," Shania said, restraining the mirth, not wanting to embarrass him.

"Better?" he asked, shoving his hands into his pockets.

"Yes," she answered, then kissed his cheek. "Thank you."

"Ready?" She held out her hand. He placed his tiny fingers against her palm.

* * * *

"Justin's a natural. It helps that he's articulate and can speak about art." Monsieur Barrett handed her a glass of champagne. Elevator music played softly in the background, currently Celine Dion's *My Heart Will Go On*.

Shania glanced around the gallery. Oil and acrylic paintings from body parts to landscape lined the walls. Metal, ceramic and other mediums held places on pedestals or directly on the floor. The charcoal collection, sectioned off due to the nature of the art, was in a separate room.

Megan stood guard over Justin. Shania and Monsieur Barrett entered the space where Justin's work was displayed. The studio owner, Jim Caraway, ran in front of them almost tromping on Monsieur Barrett's toes. Caraway ran his bony hand through his equally thinning hair. Spikes of gray wires stood on end.

"I need to talk to you about the miniature charcoal. It's signed J under the books, and the name on the contract is illegible. We have an offer of two thousand dollars for the sketch." He slapped the sides of his face. "Can you believe it? Immature work but excellent in its simplicity."

"The work is magnificent," Monsieur Barrett replied.

"Then tell me where the artist is, and I'll present him with an offer." He clasped his hands together. His loafer shod feet shuffled forward and backward. Tassels on top of his shoes bounced from side to side.

Monsieur Barrett looked at her with eyebrows raised. "Let's wait until the press gets here."

Two thousand was a lot of money for an unknown artist and a small charcoal sketch. Good heavens, the amount was so large if added to her savings, she and Justin would be set for the next year. She could graduate debt free. No, she couldn't sell her son's first drawing, Justin was proud of his work. He expected it to be placed above the television. She couldn't sell his charcoal just to make her life easier.

"I can't sell it," she stated.

"Are you the artist?" Mr. Caraway bristled to the point the few white hairs on his chin stood at attention. The curator's short stature didn't stop him from looking down his nose at her.

"No, my son is the artist," she added a touch of haughtiness to her voice. Who knew the country club visits would pay off? She could imitate one of her mother's friends with precision.

"I think, Miss, you should allow the artist himself to make that decision." His nose lifted into the air.

"Have at it." She pointed to where Justin currently performed his artist pose for photographers.

"He's a baby," Caraway claimed. "Barrett, when you said a young, new artist I didn't expect an infant."

"No, he's a big boy," Shania said under her breath. She smiled as Caraway marched toward Justin.

Monsieur Barrett touched her arm. "Oh, there are the reporters from Indianapolis. I'll go see them."

"I'll stay here," she replied and took a sip of her tangy champagne. *I Will Always Love You* by Whitney Houston played as instrumental music in the background. Shania shut her eyes, for a second. She'd always love Morgan. She opened her eyes.

The man of her wishes stood a few feet away watching her. Green eyes sparkling, he was gorgeous outfitted in a black suit. A Jerry Garcia tie with splashes of gold and cerulean looked sharp against a white shirt. The slight lifting of his lips jolted her. She touched her throat, trying to stop the fluttering lodged there. Her hand quivered, slopping the liquid against the glass. Instead of Justin's handprint on her cream dress, golden liquid would spill over the garment.

A waiter passed. She placed the flute on the tray, then took a step toward Morgan and another.

Morgan met her mid-way. "I came to tell you something very important."

She met his gaze, trying to figure out what he was going to say. Lightheaded, she tried to relax or she'd pass out without discovering his message. "Yes?"

"I'm in love with you, and I think you're in love with me." He reached into his pocket.

He said the words she'd longed to hear. "What?"

"I love you. Do you still love me?" He grinned, as if knowing she wanted to hear him say the words one more time.

She bit her bottom lip and gripped her dress to wipe off the moisture on her palms. Her heart would go on. "Yes, I'm in love with you. I've loved you since you held my hair as I puked my guts up during morning sickness."

He frowned.

"When we tell our grandchildren about our romance and my asking you to marry me could you say something else? Puke doesn't create a good image in people's minds." He wrapped his arm around her, then kissed her cheek. He tugged her to a quiet corner behind a twisted metal piece of art. Ribbons clustered at the center of the work, sprung in various directions at the midpoint. A perfect place for a moment of privacy.

Her beats per minute escalated as high as the top of the steel tower beside them, making her feel weaker yet. Shania didn't worry about falling off her high heels. Morgan held her safe in his arms. She whispered, "Are you asking me to marry you?"

"Yes, but again, let's leave that part out." His lips found hers, sending the flutter from her throat into her stomach. He broke the kiss and taking her hand into his, knelt down on one knee. "Shania, will you marry me--forever?"

"Yes, I'll marry you, Morgan Hardwick." She touched his face. "And I'll spend of the rest of my life loving you."

Meet the Author

I write because my muse demands it. Often I'll have friends or acquaintances say, "You need to tell a story about my life, it's so exciting." I've tried to create a tale from a pre-set accounting and it is like inserting needles under my fingernails. Not because my friends' stories are boring, not in the least. For me, it's difficult to base a story on what someone I care about believes is-was their life.

However, my mother-in-law is nearly blind and listens to books on tape for entertainment. She loves romances, mysteries, and stories about the military, but most of all families. Not the rich and successful trouble free families, but real people who experience true everyday problems.

Love Hurts is that type of tale. I took bits and pieces from my family and my husband's family and wove a narrative which might make you laugh, or relate, but most of all, the story may make you weep.

jj's Website:
http://twitter.com/jjKellerauthor
https://www.facebook.com/jj.keller.58
http://romancewithjjkeller.wordpress.com

Reader eMail:
justjkeller@yahoo.com